This book is dedicated to all of my friends and family that have been part of this beautiful life. While I may have lost you along the way, you remain a part of me.

In loving memory of my father.

www.mascotbooks.com

The *Magician* and the *Engineer*

For more information, please contact:
Mascot Books
620 Herndon Parkway, Suite 320
Herndon, VA 20170
info@mascotbooks.com

Library of Congress Control Number: 2018906115

CPSIA Code: PRFRE1118A
ISBN-13: 978-1-64307-089-6

Printed in Canada

the Magician and the Engineer

the
Magician
and the
Engineer

A Journey of the Mind

Michael Stone

"If a man loses pace with his companions, perhaps it is because he hears a different drummer. Let him step to the music which he hears, however measured, or far away."

- Henry David Thoreau

Contents

Introduction

I'd spent the last few years based in London. It was longer than I'd planned but I think big cities have a way of drawing you in with all their wealth and magnificence; the suggestion of hope and opportunity embodied in their architecture and history. With so many people living in apparent harmony it's hard not to feel like you're part of something important; something bigger than yourself.

I wasn't doing anything special. Like so many aspects of my life, it was chance that had brought me to London; a posting within my company that had sounded like a promotion. But the change had turned out to be less noticeable than expected and excitement was quickly replaced by disappointment.

There was nothing interesting about my work. I was just another suit working nine to five to help move the money around; a small cog in a big financial machine. I worked on commission, so the more money I moved the more I made. It was about as exciting as the expression on people's faces as we all crammed into the Underground rail system. Known by most Londoners as The Tube, it's a vast network of tunnels under London that are used well over their design capacity.

When I first arrived in London, I'd smile politely toward other passengers on my way to work. As the months went by I became one of the empty-eyed shop mannequins that surrounded me. Just like them, I stood dressed in last year's moisture-laden, wet-weather apparel, gazing at the nothing in front of me in a near catatonic state as the unventilated carriages lumbered slowly through the tunnels.

I made good money and certainly couldn't complain about my finances. I worked hard, worked out and went out. I lived in an old townhouse in Clapham Common with two bedrooms. It was wedged into a long row of identical dwellings that were mirrored on either side of the street. Its sole identifying feature was the number on the gate. And there was more than one occasion when I'd walked straight past it on my way home, unaware of my folly until I re-oriented myself by turning around.

I lived alone, which is about as much space as you can have to yourself in city life. So all things considered, I should've been happy. But somehow, with each year of blending in with all the other office workers cramming into trains, packing into endless rows of office buildings day-in day-out, I started to feel different. I started to feel empty; like the truth of my existence had slowly caught up with me regardless of my ignorance of it. Like a part of me knew the truth even if the rest of me didn't.

At the time, I didn't understand how I felt; this sense of emptiness and loss. It was like I was being slowly poisoned by some toxic gas without seeing it or smelling it, unaware of my slow demise.

I had, over the last few years, distanced myself from my past, both geographically and emotionally. It hadn't been difficult. My parents had never been part of my life even when they were. They had escaped Europe after World War II, along with millions of others with broken lives, but they had never really accepted New Zealand as their home. They were quiet and distant with me as well as with each other. I always felt like I was an afterthought in their eyes. These days I spoke to them at birthdays, but only out of habit.

I'd grown up in Christchurch on the South Island of New Zealand. It was more of a large country town than a city. It might not have been a big city, but there was always something happening. In summer we'd head to the beach if there was any surf. In winter we'd drive up to Mt Hutt for Alpine adventures. But there was always things to do even if it was just hanging out at friends' houses. My folks had always lived in the same house so I knew the neighborhood well and was surrounded by good people.

The life that I'd built in Christchurch as a young man had been all but perfect until it was permanently deconstructed when my fiancée informed me that she needed something else that I could never offer. My network of friends had seemed to vanish before me as the gravity of our break-up came home to me. Emotions that I'd never experienced consumed my thoughts as I realized the truth of what I'd lost. So it wasn't surprising that I grabbed the opportunity to move to another hemisphere and hide from a life that I could no longer face. But my time away didn't have the effect I'd intended. I was still trapped — except now I was on the other side of world, slowly fading into nothing.

I'd lost control of my mind. If we were a team, then we were like one of those married couples where whatever one says the other hears, or at least does, the opposite. There didn't seem to be any agreement in my thoughts or actions. I was trapped in this odd relationship with my mind and it wasn't going well. An underlying disharmony within me that I couldn't define nor understand pulled at me constantly. I was unable to make decisions without convincing myself they were flawed.

My mind felt stagnant and I couldn't see how to move forward. What really scared me was a vague awareness that somewhere along the way, I'd simply lost hope. Somehow I had arrived at a place in my life where I felt lost and dejected. I hadn't lost my mind — I wasn't crazy. But I was lost all the same. I'd lost my way in life and I couldn't figure out how I'd gotten there.

Some days I would turn up to work and not speak to anyone the entire day. What was even more noticeable was that when I didn't go into the office my phone remained ghostly quiet. My life was an isolated island surrounded by a crowded sea of people.

Somewhere along the way I'd changed. Whatever had been important to me in the past was gone; lost or no longer relevant. But it hadn't been like this when I was younger. I remember being a very happy child, entirely content with life. We grow up being sold the idea that "the world is your oyster" or "the future is what you make of it," and that if you work hard and do your best you will live a good life, a happy life. Maybe that's the case for some people. Maybe that's how life is meant to be. Yet I'd arrived in my future and it was suffocating me rather than setting me free. How I got there was something that I couldn't define as I couldn't explain where I was. I was ignorant ... but without the bliss.

On the weekends, I would go to the park in Clapham Common. I would read or just watch the world from my isolated vantage point. But, regardless of where I was, I always knew that I was hiding from something.

The fact is I was lost. I was in a place where I'd never been before and I couldn't find my way out of it. I'd lost the parts of my life that I really cared about, and it hurt. My journey through life had been irrevocably dissociated or dislocated from whatever meaning there had previously been in it. All I knew was that before, there was meaning and purpose in my existence but now there was just me; like when John Lennon left the Beatles behind and found Yoko Ono, only for me, there was no Yoko Ono. There was just emptiness. And in that emptiness there was nothing to replace the parts of my life that were gone.

I know it all sounds a bit pathetic. But behind the sedate, placid mask that I wore I was pathetic. I didn't see my life as difficult, I hadn't suffered any real hardship and yet I still felt lost and alone. In the emptiness that was left behind in my mind there was chaos and doubt. My thoughts were riddled with questions: How do I make the pain go away? How do I fill the hole that pulls me in? How do I give my life meaning again when everything that had been important to me was gone?

It didn't matter how I got there, into the well of self-pity I was experiencing. What mattered was that I couldn't fathom how to get out of it. It was my problem; no one else could solve it for me. My friends might pull me out of my enclave of depression when they were with me but once I was alone I'd slide right back into it, like a well-worn sofa of despair that was too comfortable to leave. I hid my feelings as best I could from those around me as well as from myself when possible. Sometimes denial is easier than facing a hard truth. It's one of those tricks that the mind likes to use to avoid facing upsetting aspects of life. I don't think ignoring a problem makes it go away. You can deny something exists, but it's still there. You can attempt to ignore it, you can pretend not to care about it, but it's always there, lurking behind your thoughts.

Friends of mine would say, "Don't worry, you'll be fine, time heals all wounds." Is that really true? Or is it just something we say when trying to support someone who is suffering? I guess time makes pain diminish. But some things mend better — and faster — than others. It's not like emptiness becomes less empty the longer you leave it.

No, I think that eventually you have to face your demons. At least you can't move on free of your demons until you face them. And, you can't face them until you understand them. But how could I understand the aspects of my life that elicited such negative and powerful emotions? I didn't have the strength to face my demons, let alone recognize their existence. Isn't that why we call them demons — because they scare the hell out of us?

I was trapped by internal conflicts that prevented me from finding happiness. Yet I couldn't face the issues of my past that had led me to where I was without destroying any strength I had left. The conflicts that were entrenched within my mind had a permanency that constantly threatened to overwhelm me. I guess some part of me knew that the answers lay in the dark recesses of my mind. And another part of me understood that I could never fully face the truth of what lurked in that darkness.

While I couldn't see how I could face my demons, that doesn't mean that I didn't face them. That's why I had to share my story, because there truly is nothing permanent but change. And my story does have a happy ending, but that happiness was only possible through understanding self.

The journey that I am about to share with you, and the incredible upheaval in my psyche that I experienced, may have been driven by my mental state at the time but it was chance that set the wheels in motion in my metaphorical mental rollercoaster ride.

My adventure started with a chance invitation from one of my good friends to a town that I will always look fondly upon: Edinburgh — a true "flower of Scotland"! How does such a rough, grey town have so much character? How can a city so bleak and grey be so colorful?

I will openly admit that it wasn't your typical kind of adventure. I'm not sure if you could market the concept as a package holiday to students looking for something to do on their gap year. But it was the most powerful experience of my life — and it was my adventure.

Some people climb Mt. Everest as their life adventure; others cross oceans in sailing yachts. I merely went to Edinburgh for a few days. It wasn't an adventure in action, it was an adventure into understanding my life. I didn't discover a far-off land or a new constellation in the night sky, I simply discovered … me.

Many of us live our lives never really fully understanding who we are. We expend so much of our time trying to make sense of the world around us but we never turn the magnifying glass the other way and try and understand the real mystery.

What if it was possible to understand the mechanics of the human mind? What if we could look inside ourselves and finally understand the circus caravan that carries us through life? Would we shy away from looking into the crystal ball or would we stare into its depths and enjoy the show?

My time in Edinburgh was a truly unique life experience. It was a grand adventure. For me, an adventure is all about how we change or grow when faced with unfamiliar problems. Hopefully we grow by not only challenging our body but challenging our mind. We learn about who we are and who we want to be. We set out into the unknown to see if we are able to deal with the challenges and adversity.

I wouldn't say I challenged my body necessarily; I wasn't the first to summit a peak or cross an ocean. My adventure was all about self-discovery, one might say the most important discovery of all, because many of the greatest challenges we face exist only within our minds.

Some adventures are planned and some we stumble into by accident. And some adventures end very differently than how they began.

There's definitely something special about Edinburgh. I felt it as soon as I arrived. It was cold and rugged on the outside, but once inside the locals were warm and welcoming with a sincerity I hadn't experienced in a long time.

I was invited up to Edinburgh by a good friend of mine in London, Simon, who was going there for work and I guess felt that I could do with a break. Maybe he was worried about me being isolated in my apartment in London, wallowing in my usual self-pity. He knew me well enough to know that I could be my own worst enemy when it came to my state of mind. He suggested I join him and said the break would do me good. Of course, escaping the stagnancy of my existence in London sounded appealing.

While my plan was based mainly around experiencing Edinburgh's "tourist trail," punctuated with high-calorie food and local beers on tap, somehow my vacation turned into something else. It evolved. And, I must warn you, it evolved in the most peculiar fashion. It would be where my emotional state would transform from negative to positive, and where I would lose hopelessness and find certainty.

It's hard to explain how it all happened. Maybe even now I procrastinate as I struggle to describe the unbelievable adventure I had while there for those few days. Dare I call it a spiritual awakening? Maybe. I was lost in life and somehow, over a week in Edinburgh, I was found.

As much as it was my adventure, this story is really about the two characters I met in Edinburgh; it's about the spiritual journey that I experienced with the assistance of these two very different but insightful people who touched my life. But I get ahead of myself.

I was off to Edinburgh for the first time, without an inkling of how my life was about to change ...

Chapter 1

Flower of Scotland

*"It is not the strongest of the species that survive,
but the ones most responsive to change."*

\- Charles Darwin

*B*ig cities have a way of hardening your soul. They prey on your natural weaknesses such as kindness, generosity, and sincerity. They teach you, through bad experiences, why you need to insulate your feelings from the rest of the populous.

I remember in my first year in London, being mugged after a stranger on the street asked me for change. My mistake was believing that change was all he wanted. Very quickly, I started seeing every pedestrian as a potential hazard that I needed to avoid when travelling to work or going to the supermarket. I would avoid eye contact with strangers and ignore almost anything that was going on in the street around me.

On another occasion a couple of years into my life in London, I was confronted by a hysterical woman who needed money for a taxi to "see her daughter in hospital" and had just been in a car accident. She was crying as she pleaded for help. I hesitantly gave her five pounds to help her out but there was a part of me that couldn't help wondering if I'd just been duped. The woman was visibly distraught; there was no way that it was a ruse.

Later, I shared my story with some friends who lived in the same area in Clapham, only to find out that she'd acted out the same drama for them a month or two earlier. I still wonder what part of her story was based on the truth of her existence; did she laugh and smile when she went home or was she trapped in some dark place like myself?

I guess like all grand market places, London had opportunities for every type. Sure there were business folk, bankers, and legitimate tradespeople from every sector. But within the framework of legal business dealings there were also the entrepreneurs of a less legal variety. Wherever naivety exists, there will be con-merchants. Where generosity exists, there will be beggars. To let your guard down is to invite a stranger in. I still love London for all that it is. But anytime I enter the city, my shields go up and I become more wary, more cynical, less trusting.

Conversely, as I made my way to the airport by above-ground train I gradually felt that I was moving away from the social battlefield that I lived in. Even at the airport just miles away from London I felt more relaxed and safe within the main terminal.

My flight to Edinburgh was quick and painless. Simon and I took the same flight. It was one of the budget airlines which meant we made the usual sacrifice in comfort for an equivalently discounted fare price. No leg room, no arm room, no fresh air; penned in like farmyard cattle. We would have been sitting separately if it wasn't for some sweet talking by Simon with the airline attendant and one of the other passengers.

"James," I heard him call out from several rows back. "I grabbed you a seat back here, mate," he said as he waved me toward the back of the plane.

Not only did he get us seats together, he also arranged a couple of cold beers while waiting for take-off as we were near the back of the plane and the stewardess appeared enchanted by his Aussie accent and charismatic nature. It's amazing what a simple "G'day luv" from him achieved.

Simon was one of those people who, as he would happily tell me, had the "gift of the gab"; he was always happy and always full of chat. He regularly befriended the people around him, whether they liked it or not. He was the perfect salesman as he combined likability, sincerity and the conviction of his expertise. This also made him a great drinking buddy for myself and all his friends, old and new.

Simon was in his late twenties, like me, and had been living and working in London for over a year. We'd met through friends and gotten along from the start. We hung out once or twice a week and it would always be him inviting me to a party or to watch a football game. He never demanded anything from me and he allowed me to hide in my dark thoughts without detracting from his mood.

Simon's jokes and stories were enough to bring anyone out of their shell. So it wasn't surprising after chatting away during the flight when the seatbelt light came on in the plane cabin and the announcement was made that we were on our final descent into Edinburgh.

When we hopped in the taxi at the airport, the driver's thick Scottish accent made me feel immediately welcomed; it kept my attention as I tried to understand him on the drive into town. There was no "big city" coldness in his voice or his words; instead he busied himself on getting to know us as we wound our way through the outer suburbs of Edinburgh towards Simon's hotel.

As he and the driver chatted away, I took in my surroundings. While the suburban streets looked similar to London, the feeling I got looking out the window was very different. While it may have been colder, temperature-wise, in Edinburgh, it felt warmer and more welcoming.

I couldn't explain what was different about my surroundings but I felt the vague suggestion of excitement. Whether it was the new city or some other instinct that stirred inside of me I couldn't tell. Even as I heard the driver say that Edinburgh was the Capital of Scotland, I felt invited by what looked to me like a small town.

Before long, we'd arrived in the old part of Edinburgh. As the taxi pulled into Simon's five-star hotel, doormen wearing kilts were quick to open his door and usher him and his luggage inside. The building was a grand, elegant old Victorian structure that made me feel like I should change my reservation.

After dropping Simon off, we headed to my more humble establishment, which was only a couple of turns from Simon's hotel. There was no doorman so I paid the driver, got my luggage, and ushered myself into what would be my home for the next few days.

I'd chosen my hotel based on photos from the internet showing the old-fashioned appearance of the outside structure as well as the large majestic entrance. The rooms had looked large, with plenty of light showering through the windows. When I entered the hotel it was clear that it was more run-down than the online images had conveyed, but it felt welcoming and cozy all the same.

I was checked into my room at the front desk by a "wee lass" who was very friendly but also spoke with the local accent that made me feel like I was hearing a foreign language rather than English. I only dared asking her to repeat herself once before saying, "Okay," or, "Thank you." I'm sure it was apparent that I couldn't understand all she was saying as I nodded and smiled sheepishly, but she was very friendly all the same and after thanking her, I headed to my room on the third floor.

After lugging my bags up the main staircase and plonking them in my room, I pulled the curtains as wide as they could go and looked down into the street below. So this was Edinburgh.

I had no notion of what to expect of Edinburgh when I was invited by Simon to check it out. I'd never been to Scotland, so the only images I had in my mind were of the usual stereotypes and clichés from movies or advertising. But now, as I stood there gazing through the window, I was struck by the realization that I was actually there. The reality of my situation finally dawned on me. Edinburgh was in front of me — with some unknown adventure beckoning me to get started!

A wave of excitement pulled at me to start exploring, and I was struck by the subconscious suggestion that I would like it once I got out there. None of my preconceptions included the sensations that I felt as I looked into the street and at the buildings around my hotel. I couldn't help but smile as the charm of Edinburgh drew me in.

Before heading out to explore the town, I flicked open a copy of *The Lonely Planet: Scotland Edition* that I'd purchased at London's Gatwick Airport. *The Lonely Planet* series is like a traveler's bible. They seem to define the tourist trail in any country you cared to travel. They provide the rules of the kiddy pool for travelers before they dare venture into deeper waters. I stashed the book and a local map in a small rucksack and headed out to explore.

My first day in Edinburgh was all about checking in to the hotel and then checking out what sights I could see within the remainder of the day. So while Simon spent the rest of the day working, I tried to make the most of my first trip to Scotland. I've always enjoyed walking and found that it gives an excellent perspective of a place. So I spent the afternoon exploring Edinburgh one street at a time, discretely inspecting my tourist map when necessary.

What a wonderful city! As I walked the cobblestoned streets I felt relaxed and at ease. There were plenty of other tourists and locals on their own missions but I felt free to explore as I please. I spent the afternoon peering into shop windows, inspecting the bars and restaurants for the coming days and eventually making my way up to Edinburgh Castle, marveling at its rugged beauty. It didn't take long before I'd mapped out most of the Edinburgh Old Town Tourist Trail.

After checking out the tourist magnets, eating the local cuisine and enjoying too many pints of liquid gold that evening with Simon and some new friends, I felt fully welcomed by Edinburgh, enticed by the potential of adventure that lay ahead.

At one point in the evening, I vaguely remember Simon convincing an on-duty policeman to sing the Scottish national anthem with us as we made our way between bars. Initially, the policeman had refrained from joining our late-night shenanigans but with Simon and I destroying his national anthem he was obliged by his sense of duty and patriotism to coach us as we discovered the passion of the Scots. My first day and the entire evening was a great start to my vacation.

When I finally made it back to my room via the majestic but incredibly long and exhausting staircase, I was in no state for anything but sleep. But after using the bathroom I made the mistake of looking at myself in the mirror. When I looked in the mirror it was like I'd come face-to-face with the truth.

My feeling of hope abandoned me as I stared. I wanted to sleep but I was transfixed by the face in the mirror. It was a sorry sight that returned my gaze. The eyes were empty as I looked into them. I tried to say hello with my eyes to the person in the reflection, but there was no response. I wanted to communicate with the face that stared back at me but I didn't know who he was.

"Hello," I said cautiously, peering drunkenly at the stranger in the mirror. "Who are you?"

There was no response. He just stared back at me with empty, unfamiliar eyes. It scared me that I didn't know the man looking back at me. I was sure that we used to know each other. I'm sure there was a time when I looked at those eyes and there was understanding between us. As I felt myself wobbling, I said goodnight to the stranger as he walked away from me and I literally stumbled into bed (as my shins would remind me the next day).

I lay my head on the oversized hotel pillow and without finishing my train of thought, I was instantly asleep. It was a deep sleep — one might say ":comatose" — as I felt myself trapped in the pitch-black cavern of sleep.

Chapter I

The Dream Weaver

"A dream is but an idea left to roam the imagination free from the confines of reality."

-Anonymous

Somewhere in the dream of a fairy tale there exists a town. It is a small town nestled, or possibly trapped, deep within the rolling hills of an ancient land. It's a quiet town, with the icy cold keeping most folk indoors. It is both lonely and alone. The most activity one may see comes from smoke rising from the blackened chimneys of crudely built cottages strewn on either side of crooked dirt streets.

The people, though rarely seen outdoors, are quiet and solemn; hardened by the nature of their existence. As a rule, they keep to themselves, suspicious of life itself. Even the dogs are silent and steely-eyed as they timidly patrol the empty village streets looking for something around the corner yet finding nothing.

It is a place where few choose to venture from and even fewer venture to. The town remains isolated from the outside world; isolated from its past as well as its future. It had always been this way. Only the occasional trader comes through bringing news, supplies and the occasional delivery from the outside world. Rarely does he leave with anything to share elsewhere.

On one such occasion, among the usual items that he delivers to the local merchant, there is a box. There is nothing special about the box. It is typical in both size and nature; a wooden crate lacking any markings other than a large black

burnt into the wood like a brand, and centered on the top side.

The only mystery one might note would be the unknown contents of the box itself. But neither the trader nor the local merchant care for such details. It is not their place to ask questions or take interest in other people's affairs. They exchange items along with their commission and their dealings are complete.

Soon the trader disappears down the main street in the opposite direction from which he arrived, continuing on his way, happy to be moving on. Then shortly afterwards, the merchant closes his store and leaves via a different smaller road.

As he travels out of town with the newly delivered wooden crate sitting in the back of his cart, his mind is not focused on its contents. Instead, he is concentrating on making his way deeper into the hills along this little-used dirt road, a road with which he himself is barely familiar.

It is not often that he comes this way to make such deliveries but he recalls just enough to find his way. The road is hardly more than a trail clinging to the sides of the hills, but it is where he must go to deliver the box. He knows of no one else who travels this road, nor has he ever seen anyone travelling on it. Yet he follows his instructions all the same. He can see from the markings in the dirt that no one has been on the track since his last excursion into this part of the hills.

While his heart is hardened and his will resolute, there is something about this trip that disquiets his soul as he travels deeper and deeper into the hills. There is a feeling he gets in this part of the land that leaves him hiding from the strange thoughts that bubble up from the dark recesses of his mind. He doesn't know why this scares him. He only knows that he will not be at ease until he has returned to the safe sanctuary of his village.

He leaves the box at the only set of gates on the unused road. As he places the box on the ground and takes his fee from beneath a smooth black stone on the gate post, he notices that the gates remain half open, the lower edges dug into the ground, unchanged from his last delivery. There are no markings in the dirt, no footprints or tracks in the dirt to be seen, yet his previous delivery has been removed at some point in his absence.

There is something about this place that doesn't make sense. Mystery hangs heavy in the still air, floating like the low-level mist that creeps through the valley. His uncertainty leaves him feeling colder than when he arrived. He is alone and yet he feels as if his movements are being watched. It is an unpleasant feeling that he experienced each time he comes to this particular place.

As he turns to leave, his eyes scan the area cautiously. He is unable to see any sign of a dwelling, no smoke rising from behind the hills, no hint of life at all. This is a place that would create fear in even the most hard of heart. A coldness envelops the merchant as unanswered questions haunt him.

After climbing back onto his cart, he heads back the way he came and it is not until he arrives back in town that he starts to relax, knowing that he is home once more. His work is complete.

Back in the valley with the half-open gates there is quietness once more. Any life that exists there is hidden below ice and snow or tucked into the rotten undergrowth. Any color that might have existed in the landscape has been scared away from this bleak and lonely place long ago. The trees are barren, with few leaves, and large pieces of bark can be seen flaking from their trunks. It is hard to tell what is alive and what is dead.

But if one continues into the hills along the untrodden path past the gates, over the first hill, and around the next, one would find a strange and ill-formed dwelling. It is little more than a shack with the look of a small, half-ruined fort or dilapidated guard tower jutting out from the side of a rocky cliff face; perhaps a defensive post from long ago.

A roof, of sorts, covers the dwelling. It looks makeshift and worn, as if it was never meant to be permanent. Yet snow, fallen branches and heavy green moss lay atop its surface, proving that is has remained unchanged for some time. A small chimney protrudes from the roof with little more than a wisp of smoke snaking out from within only to be lost in the cold winter air. It is a forgotten place in a forgotten land.

There is little life or light to been seen through the windows. It is not without stepping inside the lonely hovel that one may find a solitary candle flickering in desperation, fighting the cold air to stay alight. There, in the dim light of the candle, a solitary figure sits hunched over by the fireplace, deep in meditation, unaware that the fire is all but extinguished.

He is alone, but there is nothing lonely about him. Cloaked in mystery, illuminated by wisdom, his life seems stranger than fiction. Even in the isolated blackness of his existence, he thrives. His life is more mystery than imagined; more metaphor than mystery.

With his legs crossed, he sits silently in a large leather lounge chair. His clothing, like the chair, is worn and weathered. His face is emotionless but not without feature. He has dark, disorganized silvery hair. With his mouth closed and lips dry he sits, transfixed and immobilized, by thought. His eyes are dark and distant, his thoughts concentrated while he ponders the meaning of his existence.

But these abstract thoughts are not new. Each concept he proposes is well-tested. Each truth he recites is more mantra than model. While his existence is riddled with uncertainty, he also knows the true meaning of certainty. He knows that change comes through action. But he also knows that not all action results in progress. That's why he comes to this timeless place. It is a sanctuary from change.

While many in the new world busied themselves looking for happiness in life, he has chosen a different path. Yes, he knew the truth. He knew that much could be gained through thought alone. Was thought not a type of action? With action, one could change one's environment. With thought, one could change self. Surely any change created by self was an action of sorts, was it not?

But this wasn't the time to change environment ... that would come later. This was a time to analyze self; to question self; to change self through thought alone. Every detail of existence demanded meticulous planning. Later, he would commit to the application of his elaborate designs. However, before deciding on and taking action, he must be certain of how to act.

He knew that if he was going to experience success that he must be so in tune with his spirit that he would be conscious of every detail of his existence. Before action, he must recite every word that he desired to use. He must explore every motion he intended to display. He must imagine every nuance he wished to share. When it came time for action, even inaction needed to hold purpose. That is what his audience will demand from him.

Whether it was through the study of his mind or through the actual practice of his art, it made little difference to him. They were one and the same. His imagination was limitless. And he knew through a life of solitary training and study that anything which he could create in his mind he could make reality. If it was his wish, they would be one and the same. That is what defined him. If he could not turn thought into action, then he must accept failure as part of his life. The very idea was so dangerous that he would never let it enter his thoughts.

He was alone with his thoughts but he wasn't lonely. The idea of loneliness would be ridiculous to him if it ever entered his mind: that there could be a desire, no, a need, to be with others to attain happiness. It wasn't that he didn't need the company of others. He just had no use for them. He'd always been alone. He had no need for company. Not here anyway; not in this place. He was here to be alone with his thoughts.

No, when he desired the company of others, he would find them. But this was a time for meditation. And so he passed his time in silent repose, building and sculpting his thoughts like any artist: repeating, revising, creating, discarding, recreating.

Much had changed since his last expedition into the world beyond the hills, as it always did. But he knew well from his years of experience that if he didn't focus on perfection, if he didn't teach himself faster than the world itself changed around him, then he would become nothing more than a memory lost in time.

Memory. That was one of his greatest tools; a gift, really. Yes, practice and methodology were crucial to his success. But, it was his incredible memory that allowed him to perform the great feats for which he was known. His memory stretched back to the very beginning. It wasn't that he could remember the very day he came into existence. No, but he certainly remembered the first thing he ever learned.

He remembered learning to control the many parts of his body and not just the movement of limb and muscle alone. He was able to control much more, both consciously and unconsciously. He'd learned this high level of mental dexterity long ago.

For example, his powerful, peculiar skill allowed him to

control his heart rate; he could increase it or decrease it at will. If he wished, he could even cause himself to faint or appear dead ... but he saved those tricks for special occasions.

His ability to control his eyes was most unique; he was able to look in different directions at the same time. But not only that, he was also able to dilate his pupils individually, and at will — a most unnerving act if you happened to be the one holding his gaze when this occurred. It was like he was hypnotizing you as his pupils oscillated in and out.

He could give himself goosebumps just as easily as he could the audience. He could break out into a sweat or make his hairs stand up just through thought alone. He wasn't entirely self-taught in these arts but he was unique all the same. Yes, he remembered every trick he'd ever learned.

But his incredible memory wasn't limited to simple manipulations of his body. He was able to recall anything that he'd ever used in his act. He remembered every word he'd ever spoken. And with every experience in his life, with each and every encounter, he retained more and more detail. It was like he was constantly increasing the infrastructure for understanding within his own thoughts. These days, he was aware of even the most miniscule and inconsequential detail within his existence.

Yes, memory was what he built all his performances upon; memories of his past success. Memory itself, however, is static: The world, his world, was constantly in motion. What pleased the audience one night may irritate them the following. But he'd learned from experience that without imagination, the illusion of magic became just predictable trickery very quickly.

There were occasions — not many, but some in his past —

where his miscalculations had resulted in disastrous failures. To such an extent that he still refused to revisit these places. These mistakes were made long ago in the early days; days that he could not forget but instead were locked deep in the darkened recesses of his mind.

There must always be something new to give the audience. That was certain. There must always be an elevated degree of complexity if he was to achieve success. He must always be at least one step ahead of them. While he knew that perfection was absolute, he also knew that to succeed there must be constant change. Whether he knew it or not, he was driven by this innate instinct to succeed.

Finally, after an unknown period of time in thought, he knew what he had to do. Of course, that was the reason he came to this place. It wasn't until he removed himself from the world that he could understand it. Here, in this strange place, he was free to study his art. Here, where eternity could pass in a moment, he was free from constraint.

Through meditation, he was once more ready to face the world. With his plans finalized and the script written neatly within his mind, he was certain once more. He allowed himself a small smile of contentment to play across his face, as if to acknowledge he was ready. And then, without warning or notice, he was gone.

The man in the chair had vanished. The candle flame was replaced by a weak wisp of smoke, the abandoned fire little more than warm ash. For an instant, a small red bird with blue tips on its wings could be seen landing on the rooftop of this strange winter refuge ... but it, too, disappears from the valley.

The half-open gate in the valley remained unchanged in

the cold stillness of dawn. The box marked with a large black m was gone from the gate — but not forgotten. It had been accepted, embraced, and now was in its proper place. Only one man understood the meaning of the box. Only one man knew its value.

As the valley fades away into the distance, the rolling hills disappear, one by one. In the town lost among the hills, the stone-faced merchant can be seen locking up his store for the day. A lone dog barks timidly somewhere far in the distance. A layer of thick fog begins to envelop the land until all that can be seen is a dense blanket of clouds.

And then there is nothing.

Gone is the man from the dream of a time in a faraway land. Gone is the dream of the man — so real at one time, so clear for a moment, and yet so hard to re-capture. And as the dream fades into little more than a hint of a memory, consciousness returns.

Chapter 2

Riddle on the Hill

"An idea is like a virus. Resilient. Highly contagious. And even the smallest seed of an idea can grow. It can grow to define or destroy you."

-Inception

I woke up alone and hungover. We'd had a few pints. I think there might have been some shots of tequila as well, but at that moment I couldn't think, let alone try to remember.

My memories from the night before teased me as details popped into my mind, only to vanish before completion. I wasn't ready to face the day. I was full of the usual emptiness and hopelessness, with the added bonus of a hangover adding to my cocktail of depression. I was in a fine state. I didn't want to do anything. I just wanted to escape from my own depressing thoughts. I wanted to escape from my own head — impossible as it was.

My hangover brought with it my insecurities and negative memories. It's like my subconscious mind saved them up and then released them on me when I was at my weakest and most vulnerable, just to punish me for my poor decision-making from the previous night. I felt small and insignificant, even more than usual.

So I got myself organized and stepped out from the empty, but safe, sanctuary of my hotel room and set out into the chaotic busyness of the streets. I desperately wanted to escape the negative thoughts that filled my head but wasn't sure where I could hide from them or how I could keep them from bringing me down.

As I wandered around the old parts of Edinburgh I noticed that it didn't look (or feel) as friendly as the previous day. The pavement looked dirtier than I remembered. My eyes were drawn to cigarette butts and other litter on the cobblestones, a broken storefront window, old paint flaking off building walls. But it was even less pleasant when I studied the other pedestrians. I felt like they looked back at me with distrust, like they knew something about me that I didn't know about myself.

I was sure it was all in my head, however, between the brightness of sunlight and the eyes of the other pedestrians I was beginning to question my decision to leave the hotel. I wanted to hide and not just from myself. I increasingly felt the need to escape the socially interactive environment that only impressed upon me my own emptiness, vulnerability and dislocation from the world around me.

Looking for a sanctuary away from other people, searching for a temporary respite and escape, I found myself drawn to one of the hilltops situated in what looked like a park area. A long jagged rock face jutted out of the landscape. It looked isolated and peaceful. I don't quite know what it was that allured me to it. I guess I was looking for something to lift my mood, something to inspire me, maybe where I could be alone with my thoughts. I didn't really have a plan, but Arthur's Seat, as this particular peak is known, looked enticing.

Arthur's Seat is a patch of weathered green hillside with a sharp, rocky cliff on one side, located within Holyrood Park. It looks almost like it's been forced up out of the earth on one side, like a giant cheese wedge laying on its side — only instead of cheese, just weather-beaten grass and rocks push through the surface. It looked like a good place to get a view of Edinburgh.

Before I'd really formulated a plan, I was halfway up the hill, my legs moving me instinctively in the right direction even before I'd told them to. It's funny how sometimes you find yourself doing things before you've decided whether you want to do them or not. It makes you wonder who's making the decisions sometimes; as if the guy in the back seat is driving.

I was trudging along up the hill. Where I would end up is something I'd not yet determined. There's something healthy about walking, and I'm not talking about the exercise. There's something about walking that's therapeutic — almost meditative — because your mind takes a stroll at the same time. So with no schedule or great purpose other than going for a walk to clear my thoughts, I felt my mind, like my body, was free to wander.

And wander it did.

Before long I found myself sitting on the rocky hilltop,

looking out over Edinburgh and the local highlands. I may not have been at the very top, but I was high enough to get a great view of the surrounding area. I'd found myself a nice spot right on the edge where I could see the world but where the world couldn't really see me.

A light breeze blew, and from where I was sitting I would have ample warning if there was any rain coming. I looked all around me, trying to soak in the natural, rugged beauty of the place. It felt as if everything I laid eyes on was tough, resilient, determined to remain here, determined to survive. It reminded me of some of the locals I'd met the previous night. Everything around me had been hardened by this place. The rocks, the grass, even the town of Edinburgh looked like it had been battling the harsh weather for centuries.

I gazed out into the distance toward the horizon and tried to capture as much of the view as I could. I tried to use my surroundings to lift my spirit, clutching desperately to find some positivity, but as usual, my thoughts were troubled and uneasy, like the sense of bad weather looming on the horizon.

My eyes wandered lazily from house to house; past cars, roads and fields. I could see small ships in Edinburgh harbor but they didn't hold my attention. I scanned the horizon and inspected the darkening clouds. After some time my thoughts, like my eyes, started to drift. What was I thinking? Was I searching for something? Did it matter what I found? I was lost in thought — trapped was more like it — asking questions without being able to reach any answers.

While I was looking out from the jagged clifftop, my gaze began to focus inward, toward my own incomplete thoughts. While my eyes looked out into the distance, my mind looked inward. Once I'd settled into this new-found sanctuary on the hill, I looked within for something undefinable. I don't know whether I was asking questions or just looking for answers. But I was definitely not paying attention to where my eyes were set.

My thoughts jumped all over the place without direction or longevity. I tried to focus on abstract ideas that I felt important, but they would disappear like ghosts before I could understand what they meant. So many of the feelings we experience in life are fleeting and barely understood. How do we resolve issues that we can't begin to define? How can we deal with truths that we're too scared to admit exist?

I tried to ask myself what was it about my life that made me feel so helpless. Why did I feel this way? I'm not a melodramatic guy, but I'd dealt with my fair share of difficulties in life. For some reason I just couldn't seem to raise myself up to the challenge of life any more. I kept bombarding myself with unanswered questions: *How did I lose hope and why couldn't I get it back? What was the meaning of it all? Where was my place in life? Would anyone really notice if I was gone?*

Don't get me wrong: I wasn't suicidal. I was only sitting there to clear my mind and to appreciate the view, but the unanswered questions continued: What was my role in this world in which we exist? What was the significance of my life? Question after question consumed my thoughts.

No, I wasn't trying to escape from life, I just couldn't figure out what I'd lost or what I should do to find it. I knew I was missing something important in my life. I'm sure I'm not the only one who has at some point felt like there is a big hole within their lives. But I couldn't define the emptiness inside of me. How could I make sense of such a vague feeling?

As I looked out from the rocky outcrop, my thoughts

wandering, I felt a hint of positivity drifting through my thoughts like a gust of wind blowing through my hair. What is it about a beautiful view that lifts the spirit? Maybe it was the peace and quiet, or the escape from the claustrophobia of city life; maybe the sense of freedom we get from being able to see in all directions without impediment; or maybe the real sense of hope we get from looking, quite literally, at new horizons.

There is something special about sitting on a hill or mountain peak and looking out onto the world around us. There's something indescribably powerful about seeing so much of the world at once. Just sitting there seemed to lift — and settle — my spirit.

The weather was overcast and the clouds continued forming into a thick blanket, but occasionally the sun would peek through in a way that allowed me to witness a brilliant piercing light show as it filtered and flickered in hazy rays of light. It would last minutes or even seconds before the sun would be swallowed up by a gang of clouds, as if they had spotted a weakness within their thickly woven fabric and were determined to push together to seal it up.

It was during one of these brief flashes of light that a stranger approached from the hiking track. There had been a mix of hikers, joggers, and tourists that had passed by at a distance along the track, but they had all moved on. This was the first person to veer off the track anywhere within my vicinity.

I couldn't really make out the figure too well, as the sun was too bright at that moment and it was positioned right behind him which made it impossible to look directly at him without closing my eyes. He was probably just another hiker wanting to take a quick break from walking to check out the view, I thought.

But he ambled up to the precipice maybe as close as ten feet away from me and sat down. Immediately, I felt uncomfortable with his presence. The distance of ten feet may not seem close, but when you're the only one around and suddenly someone else is right there beside you, you notice the intrusion. I did anyway.

It was just a little too close for me to feel like I was there by myself anymore. I wondered what had just happened. I was all alone before, and suddenly, this stranger arrives. Something didn't feel right. *Find your own spot*, I thought to myself, but he hadn't broken any rule. How could he know that this was my space? I wanted to be alone. I clearly came here to be by myself.

How peculiar it was that even though I felt so lonely at the time, I still disliked the idea of anyone coming near me. I was lonely but also wanting to be alone. He wasn't even that close. I wasn't sure whether I was angry or upset with this man. It was just that before I was alone with my thoughts and now he had somehow intruded, and he probably had no idea the effect his arrival had on me.

I didn't look directly at him, but he was in my peripheral vision. I think he was looking out into the distance like me. Maybe he was doing some pondering of his own. Maybe he was depressed. Maybe his life was really bad. Maybe it was worse than mine. Yeah, maybe his life made mine look good. The idea seemed to comfort me, but I think I just wanted to pick on him as he'd interrupted my thoughts.

I tried to get back to focusing myself on focusing on myself. I attempted to re-acquire solitude in my thoughts. I looked back out into the distance trying to find the place I'd been in my head before he arrived.

When did I lose hope? I used to be so happy and care-free. When I was a kid, there was nothing that could ruin my day. I was all smiles and always happy. I'd been like that since I could remember. You couldn't break my stride, or bring me down; I was happy-go-lucky. So what had changed and how could I solve this riddle when I didn't even know what the riddle was?

I think I was there, alone with my thoughts. I was back to that place I'd found where I could ask myself lots of questions without getting any decent answers: lots of pondering but very little productivity. And that's when the stranger stole another piece of my solitude. He started speaking without any warning:

"You're looking for answers aren't you?" he asked with a Scottish accent.

I turned to look at him, but he kept his gaze trained on the view of the horizon.

"What?" I blurted out, startled and self-conscious.

"You're looking for answers … out there!" he repeated with more confidence, pointing towards the horizon.

"I'm not sure what you mean," I replied cooly, feeling very anxious and on-edge in both a metaphorical and literal sense.

"I come here quite often," he said, changing his position slightly to talk to me, "and I've found that the people who are 'soul-searching' tend to look out into the distance without focusing on anything specific. They have a 'look' about them. Well, you have that look, if you don't mind me saying," he finished conclusively.

I was quite confused. "Soul searching or looking for answers? You said both," I asked, searching for clarification.

"Soul searching, looking for answers, pondering the meaning of it all. They're all variations on a theme," he said. "It's all about finding answers to some puzzle that you need to solve within yourself," he continued, gesticulating with his hands in a way that only increased my uncertainty.

As uncomfortable as I was, his insight into my mental state intrigued me, as if this keen insight hinted at some unspoken wisdom.

"So, was I right? Is that what you were doing?" he prodded, repeating his previous question.

"Uh, well, I was, I guess," I fumbled, feeling very uneasy and uncertain of myself, if not plain vulnerable.

He chuckled, as if to acknowledge that he'd guessed right. Or was it a snort of derision? I couldn't tell. I swallowed, realizing my throat was dry, which only seemed to emphasize how uncomfortable I now felt in this stranger's company.

Who *was* this guy and what did he want? First of all, he'd invited himself into my comfort zone and then he'd decided to intrude on my thoughts with his words. I felt very awkward. If nothing else, living in London had taught me to be polite but wary. I always tried to avoid interacting with strangers. I tried to distance myself from him without actually moving, which was tricky, as you can imagine. I think I just looked at my feet rather than at the view or towards him. Not the best technique, I'm sure.

He chuckled again and continued speaking as if we knew each other; as if we were old pals:

"Why do you think it is," and he paused to take in a deep

breath, "that when we're looking for answers inside our mind we gaze out into the distance?"

"I don't know," I said with an awkward chuckle, more out of an attempt at politeness rather than finding anything funny.

And that was it. He turned his attention into the distance and, just like that, our brief conversation ceased. He didn't say another word. I didn't have anything to say. It had all lasted about as long as one of the momentary light shows the sun was performing every so often through the clouds. It came and it went.

Even though he'd stopped talking to me, I now found it entirely impossible to ignore his presence. He wasn't only in my personal space but had now transgressed into my mental space. How could I return to my internal monologue with him sitting there at my periphery, not knowing when he might speak again and ruin my dysfunctional meditation? It felt almost like my mind was attempting yoga with its thoughts but my mental poses were looking more like something out of a game of Twister.

I wanted to leave but at the same time didn't want him to think that he'd made me uncomfortable. He hadn't been rude but if I left now I felt like it would be me who was being rude. How does that work? I was in a right pickle! I didn't know what to do. I didn't know how to escape my discomfort.

Eventually, I felt my only option was to say something. I felt like either I had to talk or I had to leave and I'd already decided that it may appear rude if I walked away after he'd just spoken to me. I'm not the sort of person that enjoyed being rude to a stranger who had done nothing to me. Sure, he'd intruded on my personal space but I didn't believe it was intentional. How could he know how uncomfortable I felt? So, before I knew what words were coming out of my mouth, I asked him:

"So, does it work?"

"What do you mean?" he replied after a brief pause.

"Do these people find the answers that they're looking for out there?" I tried to clarify by gesturing towards the hills in the distance in some clumsy, self-conscious fashion.

"Ha, I don't know!" he answered with a shrug. "It's not like I can see what's going on in their minds. I just look at their eyes." He shrugged again before continuing.

"You can see it in the eyes when they are looking at something in the distance, but not focusing on it. No, I'd have to be some kind of magician to know what other people are thinking," he said.

For some reason, the word "magician" really seemed to resonate within me. The word seemed to echo within my thoughts without me knowing why, like a pebble that had been dropped into the waters of my thoughts, generating waves that rolled ceaselessly outward.

There was something in his eyes that made me feel like he wasn't sharing everything he knew, like he was holding something back, a hint of a mystery. He really was very different. He was cheerful and awkward in manner at the same time. Not someone I'd chose to talk to if I was given any option and yet I found myself wanting to ask him more questions, drawn into the very conversation I was trying to avoid. You know, there are some people that display a mix of ambivalence and certitude that makes them seem like they have all the answers. He had that aura, like behind those mysterious eyes lay the answers I was searching for. That's the sense he gave me anyway. I decided I'd challenge him to see if there was any wisdom behind his words.

"So, you appear to have the answers. What do you think it's all about?" I asked, not sure how the question might be received.

He chuckled, which he seemed to do quite a bit, but he didn't say anything. He paused for some time, as if collecting his thoughts and choosing what he would say next. He gazed into the distance, but this time, with a very different look, and he remained silent.

I looked down and fidgeted. But as time passed I started to feel uncomfortable and foolish. I got the feeling that my question had sounded stupid within the context of our brief conversation. Silence started to dominate the space between us. I started to wonder whether I'd killed the conversation by asking my question; whether I'd severed this brief connection with the strange Scotsman. Finally, it seemed he was going to respond.

"You know how people get lost?" he asked rhetorically. "Do you want to know how people find themselves sitting in your shoes, looking out there while looking in here?" he asked as he gestured lazily towards everything around him and then, pointed to his head. As I started to nod he pointed at me and said with conviction:

"They forget where they were when they started."

He nodded as if he'd said something of meaning. Now it was my turn to chuckle. But it was a cynical chuckle.

"I've heard something like that before, you know. Is it meant to be helpful?" I asked with a measure of pessimism and cynicism.

"Maybe, maybe not," he responded, as if it didn't really matter to him.

But now he'd turned his body away from the cliff edge and was facing me full-on. As he looked at me, he seemed to take my measure carefully, absorbing who I was in an instant, his eyes interrogating me, before fixing his gaze directly on my eyes.

He leaned toward me, his eyes focused intently on mine, with bushy eyebrows that seemed to underline the meaning in his eyes, if eyebrows can underline. It was the first time that I'd really looked at him.

He was scruffy and it seemed that his facial hair had won, or was at least winning, the battle for control over his face. His hair was rugged and unkempt, like the local landscape, his eyes dark and distant.

But when he looked at me, they lost that cold, distant look. It was like he switched them on and decided to bring them to life. His gaze intensified as he seized my attention. I felt like his eyes were boring holes into my soul. Like he could see into my mind and that he already knew everything about me. There was something strange but mesmerizing about them. They were serious and yet I felt like there was some real friendliness behind his intense gaze. I wasn't afraid, but within the blink of an eye he had me transfixed.

Without uttering a word, I knew that what he was going to say was important. At the time, I considered it a sign of real charisma that he could gain my attention so thoroughly, so quickly. His demeanor had changed from a jolly, nonchalant attitude to one of intense seriousness. I was caught in some kind of hypnotic spell that he must have harnessed from my discomfort, curiosity and desperation. And then, with my complete attention, he continued speaking:

"Maybe you're lost. Maybe you're having trouble finding your way. At some point you thought you knew where you were, and now you don't."

He continued holding my gaze, and continued speaking.

"And you can't figure out what happened. Life doesn't have to be as complicated as you seem to think it is. Have you ever heard the saying: 'Don't worry, it's all in your head'?" he asked rhetorically.

"You just need to understand yourself better, that's all. And, in the end, it is you who must find your way. Having said that, I have to say I like you, you make me chuckle. So, maybe I can help you. At least, maybe I can get you started. So, let me try something different. Let me tell you a secret."

Transfixed, I waited for him to continue, which he did.

"It's something I've known for a long time and I've never shared it with anyone. I've kept it to myself for longer than I can remember. It's my little secret — one of them anyway. It's a wonder that I've never thought to share it but it may just be the answer to that mysterious question that you can't quite figure out."

He paused as if to let me absorb the importance of the moment. I wanted to ask him why he would share such a secret with me or maybe thank him for doing it, or maybe even tell him that he was wasting his time, but his eyes had me trapped like a rabbit frozen in front of a car's headlights.

I was so absorbed by the insight he seemed to display and his curious manner that if someone had pushed me off the cliff right then I would still have been wondering what he'd say next as I hit the ground at the bottom. And so he continued:

"It won't make sense to you right now, or tomorrow, or the next day, but what I'm about to tell you is better than any answer that you might find out there in the distance in the clouds or on the hilltops or in the laces of your shoes that you've been staring at," he said, smiling, more to himself than to anyone else.

"What I'm about to tell you is at the core of everything you've been pondering, if I can be so presumptive to say," and this time he shared with me a little dry smile.

He paused, turning his eye briefly over the local landscape. For some strange reason as he turned back toward me the hairs on my back began tingling in anticipation. I could feel the pounding of my own heartbeat. Not to mention my mouth was still completely dry. At that moment, I was desperate to find a solution to my situation, and I wanted to believe that he could give me some unique wisdom that would save me from this quagmire my mind was in, that I couldn't help but listen.

Why is it that when you've lost all hope you tend to grab at anything that might save you? You become more desperate. A drowning person might reach for help from floating debris, a bird or even a crocodile, rather than lose grip on life. I would accept whatever help I could get even from some strange man on a hill, and he had my complete attention. No one else had been able to help me. It was like we were in our own little bubble in space and time, and everything else had faded into the distance. Like a slow motion scene from a movie.

And all he said, with his eyes fixed on me, speaking slowly and deliberately, with his curiously jolly manner, was:

"All actions are taken to increase certainty."

That was it. I remember the words as clearly as if I'd been

told them today. As he said these words, his gaze seemed to look further and further into my soul. There was a moment of emptiness where I didn't seem to understand, maybe I experienced fear, and then my mind was hit by this statement. Firstly, I thought "was that it?"

And secondly, what the hell did it mean? But, like being rear-ended unexpectedly while sitting in your car at a red light, I had no idea what just happened. I could feel my heart pounding in my chest. Something about the words had caught me off guard. There was something about the statement that was affecting me. While I couldn't make sense of it, something about the words reverberated from the back of my mind all the way to the front.

My mind was going in all different directions at the same time — but now it was in a good way! Was I excited or hysterical? I tried to grasp the meaning in his words but couldn't. But still there was a sensation like electricity buzzing through my mind.

Part of me felt incredible joy, like something amazing had just happened. Another part of me, ignorant of what had changed, was excited about something incredible in my future. I was trapped between excitement and joy and it felt great. It was like he'd just kick-started my mind, or plugged it back in, I just didn't understand how.

As I sat there wondering what the hell these words meant, the stranger got up without another word and started wandering off into the distance. His departure at that moment was even more inconceivable than his random unrequested arrival.

As he disappeared down the hill the last thing I heard from him was that carefree chuckle of his. I got the feeling he was very happy with himself. It was like he knew exactly what he'd just done. He had just planted a seed in my mind. He'd just given me an idea that he believed would help me. I could see why he would be happy with himself. I, on the other hand, didn't know what was up and what was down. I was by myself once but now this one thought resonated through my mind:

All actions are taken to increase certainty.

What had just happened? I kept on repeating his words in my head, whether deliberately or unconsciously. This one statement seemed to consume all of my awareness. I couldn't escape it nor did I want to. I knew it meant something because my mind continued feeling a sense of exhilaration.

Every time I said it to myself, my mind was hit by a wave of excitement and adrenaline. There was something about this statement that made me feel alive! I sat there repeating the statement over and over in my mind.

Why did it affect me so strongly? Whatever it meant, I knew it was important. Somehow, subconsciously, I felt like I knew what it meant but couldn't capture any clarity in my thoughts. It felt like he'd given me the answer to my question but I couldn't figure out (or remember) what my question was. Somehow, this stranger had just given me some secret key to my mind ...

But what had it unlocked?

As the sun started to set behind the clouds, I started to make my way down from Arthur's Seat. It was a very different walk from the one I took up the hill and I'm not talking about the trail I took. My attitude had changed. The walk up the hill had felt arduous and exhausting. But now, as I ambled down the hill, it felt like I was floating.

Every rock on the hillside track looked like a target to step on. On the side of the path the long grass had been bent over by the erratic nature of the wind. I looked for patterns, as if I might make sense of this newfound positivity and sudden sensibility. Even the faces of the hikers that I passed seemed to be more friendly. It was like I'd reconnected with the world around me.

Something incredible had just happened. Something amazing had just happened. Something had altered my mental state — and I didn't have a clue what it was. I felt the need to head back to town and attempt to rationalize my current state. I needed to calm down and try and make sense of this sudden change.

And that was it. That was my chance encounter with this rather odd stranger who somehow had invaded my negative thoughts and turned them upside down. I was excited for the first time in years. I was excited! I just had no idea why.

When I look back on my experience that day with the Scotsman, there was nothing else to it. I'd had a random conversation with an unusual character and all of a sudden, my mind was exploding with thoughts and ideas that all seemed to excite me. It was like this guy had somehow restored my hope. It was as if he'd reached into my mind and flicked the "on" switch.

And that was the magic trick! When I heard his words, my mind was so desperate to make sense of my situation that they hit me like a wave. Somehow, as if by magic, his words changed me.

How do you take someone who's lost and without hope in life and turn them around? I'd been stuck in a hole of self-pity for the last couple of years and now I felt like someone needed to tie me to the ground or I'd float away. How do you take a person from one extreme to the other like that without them even understanding how?

This man, this stranger, was like an Oracle who with the power of some ancient wisdom had somehow reached inside my head and fixed it and I had no idea how. We all know magic as something that occurs before our eyes that should be impossible. Well, he'd done a magic trick before my eyes that had occurred within my mind. And that is why I call him the Magician.

Magic comes in many forms, but to be able to transform someone from a state of hopelessness to happiness without them knowing how is a most noble and respectable trick indeed. And it wasn't a fleeting sensation. It didn't wear off. It wasn't like after watching a movie or stage show that the emotions we experience slowly fade away as we return home to our normal life.

No, this knew feeling was real; it was part of me. It wasn't like I'd experienced emotions that were simulated vicariously through watching something as a third party. My state of mind was my own. I'd taken the first step into a new life.

At the time, I thought that would be the last I saw of this mysterious stranger. Why would I see him again? It was so random to encounter him in the first place. But that wasn't the last I would see of him, nor was it the only magic trick I'd witness. But I get ahead of myself. First of all, I needed to make sense of what I'd just experienced. Not to mention, I still had to walk back into town and find a cozy bar and have a cold beer or two.

Most importantly, I had to write my thoughts down before they exploded inside my head. I was genuinely afraid that

I would lose these thoughts; that I would somehow forget them. So, I set out inspired and determined to make sense of it all. The Magician had disappeared down one of the hiking trails and I down another. As I made my way back into the Old Town my thoughts drifted, free at last, released from the constraints of my past depression, my worries fading away behind me with every step.

Chapter II

The Model Maker and the Daydreamer

*T*he Engineer rubs his eyes before putting his glasses back on. As he sits at his desk motionless, other than for his eyes which are focused intently on his latest project, he studies his work furtively in deliberate, patient solitude. While he works with many different businesses to complete his designs, he also keeps his business to himself. That is, he works alone. He is his own boss. His ideas are his own and each of his designs unique and specific to the task. His office and workshop are now empty, excluding himself and his latest completed project. He abhors clutter as can be seen in the highly organized work space that surrounds him.

He doesn't wear a lab coat, yet he has the look of a scientist all the same. He is dressed in simple, practical clothes. It is not a uniform, but his long-sleeve shirts have a tendency to be light blue and his trousers are a variety of shades of dark grey or plain black. His glasses rest on the lower part of his nose as he scans his designs for imperfections. Of course, he is unable to find any weakness in his latest project, not at this late stage, anyway. This is just one, last perfunctory review so that he can be completely certain before shipping his latest invention.

He cleaned and detailed the workshop the day before. The stainless steel countertops have all been wiped clean, polished and then buffed to a near perfect mirror finish. His tools have been cleaned, one by one, in a solvent bath, dried, sterilized and lubricated as necessary then laid out in their respective drawers, each one categorized based on size, type and function. The rubbish bin sits empty, save for a fresh garbage bag. The ritual of detailing his workspace allows his mind the time he needs to challenge the details of his project without distraction.

In a separate room, the new device sits packaged and is ready to ship out. Now, all but one of the overhead lights are off in the workshop. There is no need for him to access this area of the building for now.

He sits silently in his office adjoining the workshop. The office is not overly large but has enough room for a desk, a separate drafting table and a number of metal lockers. Everything in the office is white, excluding the laminate tile flooring. There is no mess, no clutter; everything has its place and everything is in its place.

As the Engineer gazes through the doorway at his latest project, he allows himself to feel a little pride as he briefly relishes his sense of satisfaction. Once again, he has finished the project on time and on budget. His latest invention sits complete, packaged, and ready for transport.

He doesn't know his client. His work is issued through the

agency that specializes in his type of unique inventions. He'd completed many such projects, so he was allowed to pick and choose between the jobs the agency posted online. He was known and respected among his peers. Even with all the secrecy involved in his line of work, people talked just enough to know he was at the top of his profession. And as was his pleasure, he only picked from the most interesting and unique requests.

What kind of person would make inventions in secret, only to have them shipped away without ever seeing them used for their given purpose? Only a man driven by the pursuit of logic as an ideal rather than a profession could live this life. Only a man who was committed to the design of perfection. It was his passion, it was his obsession.

The service entrance buzzer sounded, signaling the arrival of the shipping company. As the delivery man came to collect the crate, the Engineer took a moment to appreciate his design one more time. He could not see it within the box and he would not see it again after it was shipped out. Such was the mystery of his work. But he knew that his work was appreciated, as there was always more work than he could attend to.

As the courier maneuvered the box into the service elevator, the Engineer bid farewell to his design, his creation, encased inside a wooden box marked only with his trademark initial.

And just like that, his invention passed out of his world. His life, like his workplace, was clean and ready for his next assignment.

After he'd seen the courier load the crate into his truck and drive away on the external security camera, he turned off his computer and any lights that were still on in each space, locked up, then stepped out into the street.

His office was situated in an industrial part of the city. There were many trucks loading and unloading boxes and crates outside of warehouses or storefronts. Some of the small streets, he noticed during his walk, were even blocked with this type of traffic. The air was mixed with the rich aromas of exotic foods from local restaurants as well as the acrid smells of rubbish coming from back alleyways. It was a dirty part of the city, but unique and special all the same.

He didn't have anywhere that he needed to be, nor did he have a plan as to where he was going. But as he strolled from street to street, he found himself naturally drawn to the cultural center of the city. Block by block, he saw (and felt) the atmosphere change.

The shopfronts changed from dirty, graffiti-covered shutters with small entrances to elegant, glass-paned stores with gleaming fixtures, welcoming lighting and large, ornate doorways. The smells became more subtle, more pleasant. And the people around him were no longer busy workers but well-dressed shoppers idly purveying the stores that interested them.

As he stepped from one of these grand streets famous for selling all things unique and special, he found himself in the main square. He was now standing on cobblestones and as he looked around him he took in the beauty of the architecture that surrounded the square.

There was the Great Library to his left, built centuries ago when the masons were at their most skilled and powerful; the Cathedral to his right, with seven individual spires rising high above it like a royal crown. It was the tallest of the buildings, with massive wooden doors and intricate figures carved into the elaborate exterior stonework.

Across the square, he looked upon the Law Courts with their five great pillars guarding the stately main entrance; Latin writing decorated a single, huge monolith above the pillars. The words translated as "In Truth there is Certainty." And last of all he looked upon the Opera House, also known as the Grand Theatre. It was probably the least impressive of the buildings from the exterior but its personality came from within.

He didn't know how he'd arrived at the square. He hadn't been paying attention to which streets he took. Nor did he know what drew him to the theatre. It wasn't as if he'd planned to be standing there lining up for a ticket to see that evening's performance. Yet, this was where he was. It was like he'd been drawn there by some unseen force. Without him questioning why, he purchased a single ticket to that evening's Magic Show.

He loved to be entertained. He loved any type of theatrical performance. He loved being part of the crowd, watching them and joining them as they were being thrilled and dazzled by the performance. He didn't need to understand what brought him here — happiness needs no explanation.

Chapter 3

Happy Hour

"Any sufficiently advanced technology is indistinguishable from magic."

-Arthur C. Clarke

As I walked back into town, my thoughts seemed to be churning around inside my head with greater vigor than usual. The incredible sense of positive mental activity that I felt at the time was almost overwhelming, like a great cleansing flood of positive energy was washing out any negative thoughts that may have been lodged in the darkened recesses of my mind, leaving only fresh, wondrous space.

The sense of happiness about my new state of mind emanated from my core. And it was the words from my mysterious friend that had been the catalyst of change that produced this new mental state. His words dominated my thoughts, reverberating endlessly within my mind. It was like my mind was in agreement about this singular idea:

"All actions are taken to increase certainty."

But that thought was surrounded by countless questions: Who was this man? Where did he come from? What had just happened? How had he affected me like this? Most importantly, what did these words that he'd inserted into my consciousness really mean?

I was excited, I was happy, I felt like the future was full of hope and that everything would be as it should. I loved this new sensation I was experiencing! Imagine how good it felt to make the almost instantaneous transition from hopelessness, to being happy and filled with hope. Admittedly, I had no idea how or why I felt this way, but I was determined to hold onto this new feeling that had so fully energized my mind and body.

Somehow, the stranger's words connected with me. He'd blindsided me with his unique idea. And through this, I felt some inexplicable, innate connection with him. This Oracle of Edinburgh had somehow, within the space of what could only have been twenty minutes sitting together, reached down into my pit of despair and pulled me out of the abyss, once and for all.

For some reason, he'd sat down and shared his secret with me. I couldn't imagine what instinct made him feel that I would appreciate his words. Did he feel like there was a connection between us as well? He must have, because it was he who'd decided to reach out and communicate with me.

There must have been a reason why he chose me; a reason why he felt it was time to share his secret. How did he know what was going on in my mind? He'd been up on the hilltop, enjoying a scenic stroll, and had somehow reached directly into my world and flipped it upside down.

How is that possible? He seemed to understand my deepest thoughts. I needed to understand whether this was some kind of trick. Surely he could not have read my mind so easily. I've met people before who are very charismatic and capable of convincing you of anything, using your own responses to guide them in judging you. Maybe he was one of them; someone who was very good at making you believe in them.

Or maybe it was the words themselves that had affected me rather than the man who had spoken them. It's not possible that one simple sentence could change me so quickly. It *must* have been a trick of some kind. If there was magic in the words that he'd spoken, how did he know that they would help me? Why were his words relevant to me?

As I meandered contently through the streets back toward the hotel, all of these thoughts were colliding and reverberating within my mind. I was awash with some new wave of positivity. It was undeniable. I didn't know what I should do with it all. Could I talk about it? Should I share it with my friends? I didn't even know what had just happened. I decided that I had to get some paper and write down my thoughts. Maybe if I just wrote it all down, I could make sense of it later. At that time there were just too many thoughts going through my mind. I needed to get my head together.

After getting some stationery and a pen, I made my way to a local bar just down the street from my hotel. I'd seen it the day before. Like a lot of places in Edinburgh, its architectural style was a mix of old and new.

As I walked through the entrance, I could see that the dark, hardwood floor looked original and the high ceiling was decorated in a similar way to the hotel. The bar, however, was updated recently with a modern, black granite countertop, outfitted with assorted beers on tap and enticing-looking snacks.

I set myself up in a perfect little corner at the end of the bar away from other customers where I could get my thoughts together. I asked the barman for a pint of the local beer and proceeded to scribble down whatever thoughts came to mind, in whatever order, while sipping on my beer.

I wrote down questions. I jotted down ideas. I wrote down his statement again and again. Before long, I'd filled a dozen odd pages. I can't say my writing made much sense, but it was the only process I could think of to gain control of my thoughts and gather them up as they whirled around my mind like mini-tornados.

After a couple of hours of this, I started to lose steam. My excitement and adrenaline seemed to be waning. If I'd made any progress at all, it was in transcribing the chaos in my mind onto paper. I'd successfully filled up a bunch of pages with words that would not make sense to anyone else and possibly not even to myself if I reread them.

I was sure of one thing however: The Magician had given me the "answer" I was looking for. If there was any clarity at all in my mind, it was in the knowledge that this one statement was important. It was the key to something that I couldn't understand. It was the "answer"! The puzzle that I now faced was figuring out what the question was that I was asking of myself. Once again, I was pondering the meaning of it all, just like I'd done while on the cliff top, only now I was doing it in a bar while spinning a newly purchased authentic Edinburgh tourist pen around my fingers, listening to music and sipping on a cold ale.

But that wasn't the only difference I was talking about. I'd changed, I could feel the difference. I wasn't the same man as the one sitting on the hill earlier that day. Now, I was pondering with a sense of hope rather than starting from a point of hopelessness.

As I listened to the Brazilian folk music that happened to be playing in the bar, my thoughts were lifted. I wouldn't have expected to be sitting in a Scottish bar listening to folk music, but there I was. Somehow it fit the time and place. For some reason, I was enchanted by this mix of classic ballads sung in Portuguese. I had no idea what they were about or why they were being played in a bar in Edinburgh. But the music bonded with my emotional state to such an extent that I made a note of the album details so I could buy a copy later.

I had entered into some subdued yet sublime mental state that I never wanted to end. I was once again looking into the distance without focusing on anything in particular. I noticed what I was doing as I was looking through the bottles on the other side of the bar without really seeing what they were and smiled to myself as I reflected on the Magician's insights. Yes, something had definitely changed within me. Something had deepened.

The barman came over to see if I wanted another pint and while he was pouring a beer for me, he asked if I was a writer. You can imagine my reaction after seeing how little sense the words on the pages made:

"Me?" I said, with the hint of a laugh. "Definitely not!"

He looked down at my note pad as he served me a beer.

"Well, you seem to have written a short story since you arrived here," he observed.

"You know?" I said with a smile leaning back on the chair, "I don't think I've written that much since I finished school."

I paused for a moment, wishing to explain myself. "I just needed to get my thoughts on paper before I lost them."

"Well you're doing alright at it," he said with a smile. "A couple more pints and you'll have enough to take to the publishers," he joked before moving away to serve another patron.

"Yeah, right," I said politely. You'd get more sense out of a crazy person than from the mish-mash of thoughts that had just bubbled out of my mind.

I fiddled with my pen and sipped on my beer, satisfied that I was in a good place now. I wondered about the change that had occurred within my mind. Everything around me was continuing on as it had before. No one seemed to know that my world had just been tipped upside down, or rather right-side up. How was it that I'd changed so completely and yet in reality nothing around me had actually changed? I was still the same person. The world was unaffected by this new sense of positivity I'd assumed. And yet, everything from my perspective had shifted.

The barman pulled me from my reverie when he commented on my appearance:

"You look a little puzzled there, Mister," he said.

"Yep," I acknowledged in a friendly manner, raising my eyebrows in admission of my state. He seemed like a nice guy. I guess most people who work in bars are friendly by nature. Maybe that's part of what makes a good bar — a welcoming host who's willing to chat about whatever the clientele have on their mind at the time.

He was a young guy; couldn't have been much older than me. He was a little unkempt, from the two-day-old stubble on his chin to the untucked shirt peeking out from his uniform. His attire was professional but his attitude was casual, comfortable. He looked relaxed but he also looked like he took his job seriously. I could tell he cared about his work.

He wasn't busy serving anyone and was filling in the time drying a batch of glasses he'd just removed from the commercial dishwasher located at my end of the bar. He looked like a smart guy and after a couple of beers I was feeling chatty. I was definitely feeling less shy and insecure than this morning. I guess there was a part of me that wanted to share my happiness as well. Maybe he could help me. So I tried to start up a conversation:

"What's your name?" I asked.

"Rob," he responded kindly, and offered his hand.

"I'm James," I said, shaking his hand before continuing. "Rob, you know, I guess I am puzzled. I'm trying to understand something and I can't figure out where to start."

"Well, at least you're not confused!" he said quickly, looking at me with a testing gaze and a cheeky smile.

"Oh, I think I'm probably confused," I answered, a little unsure of what he meant.

To clarify, Rob continued. "Well, I don't mean to be pedantic, but you said 'puzzled' rather than confused," watching me look back at him quizzically.

"They're the same thing, right?" I said. "What's the difference?"

"Well, I'd say they're similar, yes, but I think that 'confused' suggests that you don't know how to make sense of something at all," he said and he paused to see if I agreed.

"And puzzled?" I asked.

"Well," he said looking down at the glass he was drying, "'Puzzled,' by definition, suggests you understand what the final picture is, you just don't know how to fit the pieces together to arrive at that picture. You know where you're trying to get to, but you haven't figured out how to get there yet."

"Okay," I acknowledged. *That made sense*, I thought.

He continued. "So, if you know what you're trying to get to, what you're trying to achieve, but you don't know how to get there, as in 'puzzled,' you're in a much better situation than if you don't even know what you're trying to achieve in the first place, right?" he asked, challenging me.

I had to agree. It made sense. I'd never thought about it, but listening to him differentiate the two definitions put me in a better place: I was puzzled rather than confused. It might only be a small difference but it seemed to matter.

Maybe he'd just confirmed one of the reasons why I was feeling more positive than usual. Maybe the man on the mountain had elevated my consciousness from that state of "hopeless and confused" to "hopeful and puzzled." I liked this new state of mind, and I certainly appreciated the distinctions the barman had made.

"Thanks Rob," I said. "I like that!"

"Aye, no problem," he responded affably. "I find things are always easier to understand once you break them down into their individual components."

I took a sip of my beer and wondered about the barman's last comment. He was clearly making a reference to my puzzle. His suggestion was that I should look at each piece of my puzzle so that I could understand how it all fit together.

I looked at the words on the paper in front of me again:

"All actions are taken to increase certainty."

How could I break this simple statement into pieces? They were just words on a page. I could look up the definitions of the words in a dictionary, but how would that help? I already knew what the words meant ... or so I thought.

When I spoke to the man on the hillside, we were talking about the state of my mind. His words were said to help me understand the state of my mind, to answer a question, to explain some part of why I felt the way I'd felt. Somehow, his words had changed how I felt; his words had adjusted my mental state. I felt on top of the world. So, why did I need to understand the words in front of me? I felt like it was important that I understand the message from my cryptic friend. It wasn't enough that I was happy. Sure, I could just enjoy my new found happiness. But, I felt like my journey was incomplete. I still had far too many questions and very few answers.

I now thought of my situation in the terms of a puzzle where the questions I asked were in the form of unconnected pieces and the answers to these questions were the result of connecting the pieces to form a complete picture.

It seemed like I now had a number of puzzles to consider. The first was what did the words in his statement mean? The second was how had they affected me so dramatically? The third that I could think of was why did I feel like I needed to understand them?

I didn't know the answer to any of these questions but felt positive that eventually I could work it out. Like the barman said: I knew what the picture was that I was trying to assemble I just needed to figure out how the pieces fit together. I know he probably wasn't referring to something as abstract as the human mind, or my mind for that matter, when he offered his advice though. How do you divide abstract thoughts within your mind into pieces? How do we define ideas or concepts that only exist within our mind? How do we start to understand something as complicated as the mind? Once again, I found myself at an impasse. I had too many questions and no idea how to answer them.

I decided to take a break from my perplexing thoughts and when the barman returned to my end of the bar I continued my conversation with him in an effort to change topic:

"Any chance you studied English language at school?" I asked him.

"Hell, no!" he said back. "I was terrible at English."

"Oh, okay," I said. "It just seemed like you had a background in language, based on what you said before."

"Nope, I went down a different path," he corrected me. "I'm an engineer," he said with a wry smile that reminded me for a moment of the man on the hill.

"I guess that explains 'breaking things down into pieces to explain them' when trying to solve a puzzle?" I questioned him.

"Maybe, I think we all do that, though. It doesn't matter whether you're an engineer, or a doctor, or a hair dresser — trying to solve the puzzle is what life is all about."

He looked around as if judging whether to share his thoughts with me. "I mean, we all try and make sense of complicated things so that we can understand them. It doesn't matter who you are. It's definitely what science is about and science is just the result of our desire for understanding our environment," he said, shrugging his shoulders as if to say

"Isn't that right?" or "It's not complicated!"

"I guess, maybe engineers just look at things in a more mathematical way?" I suggested, not really thinking in his terms. "So how come you're working in a bar, then?" I asked, not meaning to be rude but genuinely wanting to know.

"I'm doing my post-graduate work here at Edinburgh University. And, well, we've all got bills to pay, you know!"

Once again, he left to serve a customer. I didn't really think you could compare a doctor to a hair dresser, but I got his point. We all learn to understand what we need to understand. We all learn complicated subject matter by breaking it down and learning specific aspects of it. Does it matter whether it is learning biology or how to be a car mechanic or the art of hairdressing? To understand anything that we see as complicated, we need to break it down into pieces that we can mentally digest so that we can reassemble them into understanding the complete picture.

"Hey, Rob," I said, as he relocated back to my end of the bar, "What's the difference between an engineer and a mechanic?"

"Well, they're just job titles really," he answered. "The way I think of it is that a mechanic is someone who is employed to fix something when it is broken and an engineer is employed to understand how it works so that it doesn't break next time."

"An engineer," he continued, "understands the system as a whole based on understanding the purpose of each component as a function of the system. That's not to say that a mechanic doesn't understand how something works or why it broke in the first place. He might even do a better job at designing it than the engineer."

"Like I said, they're just job titles. Engineers tend to work in offices and focus on design or management of engineering systems. But we're all engineers in our own right," he said thoughtfully.

"How do you mean?" I asked, a little doubtful.

"Well, any time we define a problem that we need to resolve and design a solution that removes the problem, we do the same thing an engineer does. I think we're all engineers, we just focus on different aspects of life where there are problems that need to be resolved."

"While everyone thinks of engineers as the people who work on and resolve problems concerning mechanical and electrical systems — whether it's in the civil engineering or aviation, mining or manufacturing — it all boils down to problem definition based on need and how the problem can be resolved based on available means. That's the same as any profession you look at."

He stopped to see if I understood his perspective.

"But I'm not an engineer. How does that apply to me?" I asked insistently.

"Right. So you're faced with problems every day and you attempt to resolve them using your own ingenuity. A professional, in any line of work, is just someone who has been properly trained or educated in the process of resolving a specific group of problems," he said practically.

"The problems may be of a legal, accounting, or scientific nature for that matter. But they all engineer a solution based on their education and own skills. We just group engineers, as a profession, into the people who focus on resolving problems in physical systems that are mechanical, electrical or require a higher specialization in science than other professions," he said, looking at me to see if his words made sense.

"But, I don't think that applies to everyone," I responded, suggesting that he wasn't making progress in conveying his viewpoint.

"Look. You're not an engineer, and you haven't been trained as one. However, you do engineer solutions to your own problems every day. Look at the puzzle that you're trying to solve at the moment," he said, pointing at the notepad.

"The problem that you're trying to solve is how to complete the puzzle, whatever it is, given that you know what the end result will look like. You have to use your knowledge and your intelligence to figure out how the pieces of the puzzle fit together to make the picture. You have a problem that you need to solve. Engineering is the process of finding that solution. If you look at it in this way you can see that we all engineer solutions every day," he said, finishing his point.

"I see what you're saying," I said, nodding thoughtfully. Not only was he an amiable chap, he also had a way of making complex concepts sound simple. He had definitely earned his tip.

As I let this new perspective sink in, I had an idea: We all try and understand the big picture but on the flip side, a lot of people don't understand how things work. They just deal with each problem as it comes, with whatever solution they can find at the time.

If we don't look at the big picture, at the more expansive issue, how can we understand why certain problems in our life exist or how to solve them more effectively? A new idea came into my thoughts and I smiled with a sense of satisfaction.

"Maybe some of us are more like mechanics than engineers," I said, looking at Rob to see if he knew what I meant.

"Now you're getting it!" he responded, returning my look of satisfaction before moving away and waving farewell to some clientele. He may have been close in age to me, but he seemed to understand life in a way that was far beyond our years.

I wondered whether I could use any of his ideas to solve my puzzle. Surely, there was some useful insight for grasping the ideas that the man on the mountain had introduced to me. It was then that the barman interrupted my thoughts:

"Hey buddy, nice talking with you but I'm afraid I have to close up now."

"Oh, is that the time?" I said to myself as I looked at my watch, wondering where the time had gone. After I'd paid my bill, I grabbed my things and thanked him for the conversation. As I was about to head out through the door he called out to me with one last thought:

"Hey James, you certainly seem to be excited about whatever is puzzling you, so I hope you figure it out. Goodnight!"

And with that, I headed off. I felt very satisfied with myself, a mix of positive thoughts and alcohol buzzing through my mind. "What a day!" I thought to myself, and I couldn't help but feel happy with life.

I just wished I could share this sensation with someone.

I wondered where Simon had been tonight and whether I would tell him about today's adventure when I saw him tomorrow. We had a good friendship but somehow I didn't think this was the sort of thing that would interest him.

I smiled as I stepped into the hotel lobby and passed the concierge station. I was hoping to share my newfound happiness with the pretty girl behind the desk who'd first helped me check in, but settled instead with a friendly salute to the grey-haired night watchman who looked at me curiously as if he knew me from somewhere. I couldn't recall him.

Maybe he'd seen me stumble in the night before. As I made my way up the over-sized staircase to the second floor I put extra effort into not appearing inebriated. But who was I trying to kid? Let the night watchman think what he liked. It had been a truly unique day.

When I look back on this day in Edinburgh, it still intrigues me. How can a person's perspective on life change so dramatically between the course of waking up and going to bed? My mind had been "rear-ended" with some new concept that I couldn't as yet understand and I was now suffering from mental whiplash. But as my mind reeled at these new feelings, I could not help but enjoy how I felt.

It was still just a sense of a sensation rather than something I understood and could explain. It was still unclear to me what had happened. The significance of the statement was confounding me. Of course, it would be foolish of me to believe that my experience could affect the reader the way it affected me, they were not in the same place as me.

It's unlikely that you could understand what I was experiencing after being drawn from such a low place to such a high or why I felt so elated. Why did life wait until I was at my absolute bottom before finding a way to lift me back up? No, there is more to the picture that I need to paint before I can expect you to see what I saw but could not understand.

It had been a unique and special day. What surprised me even more was that the following day would have even more influence on my psyche. It felt like my mind was already up in the clouds floating above reality, high on this new wave of positivity. How could this feeling get any better?

As I lay on my bed that night gazing at the old-fashioned vaulted ceiling and the dusty chandelier, I started to relax. I'd done enough for today. I was exhausted yet satisfied with the day's events. I felt a warm glow from within as my thoughts drifted. I turned off the lights ready to embrace sleep.

In the darkness of the hotel room, my mind finally started to slow down. With my eyes closed, I started to forget the world around me. One by one, my worries seemed to fade into the distant recesses of my mind. At some point, there was just me. But as sleep took over, even that disappeared.

Sleep comes to all of us in different ways at different times. Sometimes we are unaware of the process as we fall into a deep sleep before we can even catch a glimpse of our loss of consciousness. But occasionally, the transition between wakefulness and asleep is just gradual enough that we say to ourselves, "Hold on, these thoughts don't make sense. Okay. It must be happening. I'm falling asleep."

The actual process of falling asleep feels like we are losing control of our own imagination. Our thoughts become more random, more distracted. A rule of logic within our mind has been broken, like realizing, "Hold on, spiders aren't that big; they definitely don't eat people."

Just for a moment, we recognize that something isn't quite right. It either startles us back into full consciousness or signals our last conscious thought before surrendering completely to our dreams. And without knowing how or why, we hand over control of our thoughts to some unknown entity to steer our imagination in whatever direction they please.

We relinquish responsibility for our thoughts, and in some cases, our actions. We are no longer conscious of what thoughts travel through our mind. Without any means of recognizing the change, or confirming our new state, we find ourselves, or maybe I should say we lose ourselves in this state of deep sleep.

Chapter III

The Transcendental Plain

*E*mpty plains stretch out in all directions. The plains were void of activity; bland in detail. The colors of the landscape were so pale and soft that it was difficult to tell where the plains ended and the sky began. The land was barren and dry, starved of rain and scorched by the heat of the sun, lacking in the textures that life gives any environment.

It was hard to tell if the haze in the distance was created by the heat or by the wind-blown dust. There were shapes around the landscape here and there. But they were so far away that they could have been anything: trees, rocks, maybe even a farmhouse or barn deserted long ago. There was but one road that stretched across the plain leading the way for the traveler to follow.

The coach had been trundling across the plain for a time

that could not be defined. It could have been for an instant, an eternity, or maybe both. Imagine a place where time doesn't exist. Change occurs, but there is no past or future to relate it with, there is only now.

Without the enigmatic presence of a past or the promise of a future, the meaning of time becomes more vague. In this place, time lost its relevance as did change. Moments in time exist *separated* by time but not linked by time. It cannot make sense and yet here, in this place, it does. Such is the paradox of the plain.

As the coach passed below a large cloud bank, the light began to fade. In a gradient so slight that it was imperceptible to the human eye; the view from the carriage darkened as daylight deserted the plains.

The coach moved steadily along the track as a fresh, cooling breeze swept across the plains, rattling the open windows and occasionally whipping the curtains around in unpredictable wild patterns. Far in the distance, a sheet of white could be seen hitting the ground, a curtain of a different kind, slowly consuming the plains as it approached the track.

A change was coming, bringing heavy rain to the sunburnt land. The wall of rain approached steadily until it consumed the land completely, including the isolated coach as it continued its journey across the plains outside of time but within a time.

The traveler closed the windows as the first drops of rain entered the cabin. There was nothing to be seen from the coach now except the heavy downpour of rain as it bombarded the unsuspecting barren land.

The long-slow, as the Magician referred to it, of the plains was a peaceful time; an important time. It was the connection between freedom from time and the logic of reality. It was only through crossing the plains that the Magician could maintain the duality of his existence. As each moment of time passed, the shades of one reality evaporated behind him and shades of another reality pulsed into existence, like bursts of lightning in the storm around him as he transposed between the two worlds.

The carriage was dark and quiet. Inside, the Magician sat once more alone with his thoughts. But then he was always alone. Even when he was surrounded by people, he was alone. Sure, when the fans flocked to him after each performance he would pay them courtesy, but their lives were simple and his words seemed unimportant to them.

They didn't wish to understand the mystery; they only wanted to experience the happiness and delight it produced. His subtleties were lost upon the people he tried to please the most through his art. He may have been in their presence, but he was never in their world. His world was built on rules and structure. His existence dependent on his actions alone. Theirs was a two-dimensional world corrupted by their environment. They were dependent on the external world in a way that he would never understand, and never accept, for himself. Their simplicity was obvious to him. While they derived their meaning from the world around them, he derived meaning from self.

Of course, he needed them, just as they needed him; he was perfectly aware of the symbiotic relationship. He used them just as they used him. He used them to measure his success, while they used him as an aspect of their environment; they came to the theatre for emotional satisfaction and when they came to see him, their emotions were subject to his whim.

They were like branches moving in the wind, without a will of their own, trapped in their dependency on nature itself.

But there was no one around now. Not in the carriage or outside the carriage. Such was the nature of this place. It didn't make sense, it didn't need to. Here, there was just the warm glow of a hint of change. There was the feeling, the sensation, of change without the connection to change.

It was as if each thought he had was a snapshot trapped in a moment; as if he was experiencing time through a series of shuffled photos rather than in a single, fluid sequence. Had the rain passed or was it yet to come? There were few rules in this place that made sense. It would not remain like this for long. But it was long enough for the lone man to let his imagination simulate the upcoming events.

Imagination was his dress rehearsal. Imagination allowed him the freedom to act without consequence. Imagination allowed him to live in the future without needing to step into it; with the wisdom gained through establishing future circumstance without actual consequence. Yes, even if the audience wasn't present, his imagination was all he needed in preparation for his next engagement.

As he let his thoughts play out within each carefully scripted performance, he took note of what elements of his performance he needed to focus on. He watched as an audience within his mind reacted to his stage show. He imagined their reaction. He looked from the people at the front all the way up to the people in the pavilion. He interrogated each of them with his eyes looking for satisfaction. Were they happy? Were they amazed? He planned for the best show ever, of course, but he knew that there was always the chance of failure. It was this awareness of the possibility of failure that drove him onwards. Success was never assured, it was something that needed to be carefully tended to. And while success wasn't just up to the audience they were the first indication. They were his greatest critics. They were also hard to win back if he was to lose their respect and admiration.

The audience. He knew so much about them; what they liked; what they wanted to see. He would do anything to please them. He would do everything to keep them satisfied. He recalled their joy and excitement as he performed for them. He remembered their faces as he moved from one impossible act to another. Their applause was welcomed by him but it was their delight and wonder that he strived for every time he performed. He watched each of their faces trying to measure the effect of his stage show. What was it that they enjoyed? Did any of the crowd appear disinterested? God forbid if he saw anyone talking to a friend or even worse sleeping. This was the height of failure but these days he knew how to keep them on the edge of their seats. He could hypnotize them with wonder or mesmerize them with delight. They were his puppets and he their puppeteer.

There was one member of the audience, however, that always caught his eye whose identity remained an enigma; one man in the audience who seemed different. There was something unique about him he thought as he imagined the man sitting somewhere near the back of the crowd. He couldn't explain it but there was something special about the individual. He was no reed of grass in the wind. The man had eyes that suggested something more. It was almost like he could see a depth of character in the man's eyes that was absent in the rest of the audience. And, it wasn't just one time he witnessed the individual. It seemed like he came to every show although the Magician didn't always see him in the crowd. It was as if he could sense his presence, feel his gaze, even without actually identifying him in the crowd. There were many faces in the crowd; sometimes too many faces to know all of them. So, it was no surprise to the Magician if he could not see the stranger at a particular performance. But, for whatever reason, he knew he could *feel* the presence of this stranger somewhere in the crowd.

What puzzled the Magician was his own blindness to the meaning behind the stranger. Who was he? Why was there a connection between them? If only he was to speak with him after a show, he could solve this nagging mystery. The Magician had always been a man of mystery. However, the mysteries were for his audience, not for himself. Who was this man with eyes that held such deep meaning?

But this line of pondering would not aid him in his performance. The Magician returned to his mental rehearsing as heavy rain pounded away on the roof of the carriage. Step by step, act by act, he finalized the intricate details of his next show. If he was right in his predictions, this would be his greatest show yet.

As he peered outside the coach, the rain ceased its downpour for the first or last time. As the sun hit his eyes with a brightness that was immutable, the Magician moved to protect his visibility. He knew before he could see that the plains had disappeared. He could hear the noises of the city around him. He could smell a variety of urban fragrances as they wafted into his consciousness.

And with that, he could feel the hands of time moving again. He also realized that after so many moments without time that right here — right now — was the time to act. The coach came to a stop amongst the noise and chaos of the city. As he moved his hand away from his eyes and glared into the brightness, he stepped outside into the busy crowd. Today was going to be unique. He could feel the magic in the air. Time, along with reality, was upon him.

Chapter 4

A Change In the Wind

I woke up the next morning refreshed and invigorated. There was no more hangover holding my mind captive as I got out of bed. There was no sense of depression or vulnerability as I readied myself for the new day. I was on holiday in Edinburgh and I felt great.

After meeting Simon for breakfast the next day and doing my best to contain my excitement and positivity from him, I headed out again. Of course I wanted to talk about what was going on in my head; I just wasn't sure who would be interested in my attempts to understand this new sensation within my mind. At best I might sound weird; at worst I might sound crazy.

I left the hotel that morning with a very different mindset than I had the previous day. I was no longer trying to escape from my mind, rather I was exploring it. I was searching for meaning in the riddles that I'd just discovered. And it felt good.

This time, I took with me the pad and pen from the day before and I ventured back up to the top of Arthur's Seat. My plan was to sit and contemplate my experience from the previous day and carefully record any insights. For whatever reason, my place on the clifftop had provided me with an atmosphere for change. I figured I should give it another try. Hopefully, the weather would hold out for me again.

I had a puzzle to solve, as the engineering student had suggested. I knew what the puzzle looked like from what the Magician had told me. I just had to figure out how the pieces would fit together.

I had no idea how I would resolve this conundrum of mine. Unlike the previous day, I woke that day with a sense of excitement and exhilaration buzzing within my head. My mind was consumed by a mix of positivity and unanswered questions. Better still, I knew what I was trying to achieve. I had to convert my sense of a sensation into an *understanding* of a sensation. Meaning, I knew the Magician's statement created a sensation within my mind, I could feel it; almost like I could reach out and grab it but had not yet taken this step. What I needed to do was understand why his statement made me feel this way. What was hidden in his seemingly simple words?

So I wandered up the hill again, hoping to resolve this puzzle that I had in my mind. I now walked with confidence and enthusiasm. I soaked in the beauty of the world around me. Of course the weather was overcast, but that didn't detract from the scenery. Instead, it enhanced my sense of place; my sense of *being* in Scotland.

The colors around me were weathered, like the landscape. I could see that the wind and rain had been working together, cutting away from the rocky outcrops in ultra-slow motion for countless centuries. The long grass looked like it had been beaten into submission by the wind and rain as they dueled for dominance that left the grass pointing at radical angles as if pointing towards the winner, or away for that matter.

Everything I saw around me added to the sense of being in Scotland. Everything I saw inspired me. I was in love with my Edinburgh experience. All that was missing was the stereotypical red-haired bagpiper in a kilt, standing high up on the hill, filling the air with unique haggis-generated sounds, and my morning would be a true Scottish cliché. With eyes that saw the world through this new filter of freshness and positivity, everything I saw or felt was beautiful. Life was beautiful.

I really was alive again. I now felt like I would enjoy every experience life presented to me, whereas previously, I just saw endless emptiness. I think a lot of us get stuck in life without any belief that good things are ahead of us, or that change of any sort is coming. We just learn to accept that this is the way life is — and we deal with it. But, through choice or chance, life occasionally opens up new possibilities and reminds us that there is more out there than the stagnancy of complacently that we have come to accept, that the barriers we see around us are assumed, rather than real.

Well, my eyes had just been opened to a new world, which funnily enough was the same world I'd lived in all along! I guess it wasn't the world that had changed ... it was me. I was a new me, I'd changed and it felt good! I hadn't changed in appearance, either. It was my *mind* that was different. I felt like the phoenix rising from the ashes. That's how good I felt that morning.

I ambled along various footpaths leading out of town and up the same hillside dirt trail from the previous day. As I approached the top of the park, my thoughts cleared as I focused on finding somewhere to sit. I looked ahead along the dirt path and to my surprise stopped dead in my tracks. I couldn't believe my eyes.

I looked into the distance at the silhouette of a figure that was instantly familiar. There he was, my friend from the previous day! Maybe this was part of his daily routine, although there was nothing routine about him. But there he was, sitting alone on a large rock that lay by itself on the eastern side of the hilltop surrounded by tussocks of grass, not too far from the track.

The rock wasn't that far from the precipice of the cliff where I'd sat the day before, only it was on the other side of the hiking trail. He was facing away from me and I wasn't sure whether I should approach him to say hello or leave him in peace. I was fairly certain that I could change my course and find somewhere else to sit without passing or interrupting him. I wasn't one to intrude on another person's space; not like he'd done to me the previous day. But, I certainly wanted to speak to him. No, I *needed* to speak to him. Maybe he could explain to me what he meant the previous day; he could tell me why his statement had affected me the way it had. Maybe he was waiting there for me. Regardless, I had to know how words that I thought I understood had meaning that I still couldn't as yet grasp.

I decided that this was a fortuitous coincidence and that I should take advantage of it, rather than shying away from such an opportunity. That was the old me — shy and negative. The new me saw life as an adventure, something to grab hold of rather than to let it pass me by. I had to embrace my good luck.

I walked over to him and as I approached I'd planned to say hello, but he beat me to it:

"Good morning," he said, with his Scottish accent and without turning around to look at me.

"Good morning," I responded and as I came to face him. "How did you know it was me?"

"How do you think?" he asked back, being awkward and weird as usual.

At least I knew I'd found the right guy. A picture of Yoda from *Star Wars* came into my mind saying, "How is it you think I do?" and I wondered if there was a parallel to my friend here. Was he like a Jedi Master in some way? Why is it that the wiser people become, the more cryptic they tend to be?

But I hadn't come here to understand him. I didn't need to know how he'd sensed my approach without looking. Instead, I had to engage my new friend before he decided to disappear off into the distance again.

"Do you mind if I join you?" I asked.

He waved his hand in a friendly manner and offered me a seat on his rock. At least I had the courtesy to ask if I was welcome.

"I'm James, by the way," I said holding out my hand. Again, I wished for a degree of formality or civility.

"Ha, I don't need to know your name to know who you are," he said, shaking his head and ignoring my outstretched hand.

I inhaled a large breath, raised my eyebrows and blinked rapidly, trying to move past my discomfort at his response.

He really didn't make any sense. I pocketed my rejected and awkward hand and sat on the rock with him a little lower to one side.

"So, did you enjoy the rest of your day yesterday?" he asked without looking at me.

"I did! I had a great evening, thank you. Probably had too much to drink, but I was happier than I've been in a long time. I think it was all because of what you said to me yesterday. I mean, I know it was. It's like my head was surrounded by storm clouds and overnight they've cleared. All I see or feel is blue skies. So, thank you, I guess!" I said in a happy burst, looking towards him for a reaction.

"It really was nothing you wouldn't do for yourself if you knew how. It's all about perspective," he said, again, not looking in my direction. It was like his mind was somewhere else and was only paying me enough attention to converse.

"You know," I said, "I still have no idea what you meant yesterday."

"No?" he asked, "Why's that?"

"Well, after you disappeared down the track yesterday, my mind was buzzing with what you said. I walked back into town and I sat for hours trying to find meaning in your words, but only succeeded in using a lot of ink and paper to record the list of incomplete ideas and questions in my mind."

I continued, eager to share. "Every time I thought I was about to grasp the meaning of what you said, my mind seemed to get distracted. It was like playing Pin the Tail on the Donkey and having someone keep moving the donkey without telling me its new location. Do you know what I mean?"

"I don't know, it sounds like you're making progress," he offered, but I didn't agree with him.

"Not really," I answered, "but I feel like you've told me something important. I can't get your words out of my head. I know the answer is there, in the back of my mind. But I just don't understand how to make sense of it. How can I be so convinced that your words hold insight yet not see their meaning? *All actions are taken to increase certainty'* — what does it mean?" I asked expectantly.

"Maybe it doesn't mean anything," he answered simply. "Maybe it means something different to different people. I can't tell you what it means to you, you have to work that out yourself."

I felt like he'd taken the wind out of my sails. Was he going to help me or not? I'd been so excited when I saw him there. Surely, he could explain to me why I felt as I did. Surely, he understood his own words and could tell me what they meant. I started to doubt myself, then; I started to doubt that he would be able to help me.

"Okay," I said, trying to capture the right question to ask. "How can I use your statement? What is it for? If I'm hungry, I eat. If I'm thirsty, I drink. Is that it? Is that all it means?" I asked in a slightly desperate manner.

He'd put this thought in my mind. It was only fair that he would explain what it meant. He exhaled while choosing his words carefully.

"My theory — and it is just a theory — explains everything that goes on in your head," he answered. "That's it. It's not complicated. You don't have to be clever to understand it. Everything that you think and do is based on this very simple statement. It is where thought begins."

He looked at me in a friendly way now, with softened eyes and a gentle smile. Like he wanted me to understand but he couldn't make it any simpler.

"Really?" I questioned, doubtfully.

How can a single statement explain my thoughts and actions? How can one sentence explain the human mind? It didn't gel. On the one hand, these words made me feel emotions that I didn't know existed in me and on the other hand, this cryptic fellow suggested something that just wasn't feasible.

You can't explain the human mind in a thousand pages, let alone in a single sentence. You can't explain the myriad of emotions that we feel every day in a sentence. How can words capture the meaning of something like happiness? Yet something about hearing his simple statement had made me feel happier than I'd felt in several years. I don't think I'd ever felt quite as positive and uplifted as I did now. Still, what he said didn't make complete sense.

"How can your statement explain happiness?" I asked, "How can it explain any emotion for that matter?"

"Very easily," he said, without a suggestion of doubt on his part.

But that was all he said.

He looked over my way as if "checking in" to my world for a moment, and then his mind appeared to go back to whatever it was that he was thinking about before. Was he deliberately being difficult? He suggested he had some of the most important answers to my life; an inner understanding of how my mind worked. At the same time he didn't seem to want to share them.

"Okay, how does your statement explain emotion?" I repeated, pleading with him now.

He smiled to himself. "Is it my statement? Or is it yours? All I did was offer it to you as a gift. Is it I who needs it or is it you who needs it? My words, my ideas, where do they exist? Are we not talking about your mind now?" he asked cryptically, looking at me with his dark, complicated eyes, eyes that seemed serious while also finding humor in everything that they saw unfolding.

He studied me, apparently gauging my reaction to his words.

"Emotion," he said, finally coming back to my question, "is the mind's way of telling you that there's been a change in certainty, that's all."

And then he stood up. My heart missed a beat as I thought he was leaving already. I thought he may just drift away into the distance as he'd done the day before. He certainly didn't seem too concerned with social formalities. But he hadn't finished what he was saying yet. He turned to me, with the sun behind him, dusting himself off and re-arranging his clothing.

I looked up at him without standing. The light of the sun was obscuring his features but his eyes still had a way of piercing my soul as if they owned it. I wish I knew how he did that. And once again he left me with his parting shot:

"Emotions, well, all emotions for that matter, are created by a change in certainty," he said, dipping his head, raising his eyebrows and smiling as if to say, "Understand?"

And then he was off.

There was no "Goodbye" or "Cheerio." He clearly had

no concern for social pleasantries. I don't think he even cared for conversations, but he clearly had ideas that were powerful, profound, and very important to me. Once again, my opportunity to learn from him was finished. Class was over. As I asked myself whether I'd see him again he turned as if answering my unspoken question:

"See you around, James!"

I'm sure I heard a harrumph or a chuckle as he disappeared.

I didn't know what to say without it sounding awkward so I just held up my hand to wave him off. He wasn't even looking in my direction so the gesture was only for my benefit. *See me around? Where?* I asked myself.

I hate it when people say that and you have no idea of when or how you'll ever actually see them again. As he ambled down the hill, I heard him whistling the tune from "Flower of Scotland." As with many of my encounters with this strange man, I wondered at the coincidence of him whistling a song that I'd just heard for the first time only two nights before. It was the Scottish National Anthem ... maybe that's why he liked it. The same reason I liked it. But there were so many unexplained coincidences in our encounters. I always felt like there was something I was missing. I just had too many questions in my mind at that moment to make sense of it all.

What had he said as he was leaving? I reached for the pad and pen and on a fresh page I wrote:

"All emotions are created by a change in certainty."

As if to put all my thoughts in front me, I wrote below that the statement from the previous day:

"All actions are taken to increase certainty."

I looked at the words in front of me, wondering what they meant. I tore the sheet off and scrunched up the page I'd just started. It wasn't correct. I started again on another page:

"All actions are taken to increase certainty."

&

"All emotions are created by a change in certainty."

That was better. I had to keep them in the right order. Right there on the page was the puzzle that I had to solve!

His suggestion was that my thoughts and feelings could be explained by these two simple statements. The strange thing was that something in my gut said I agreed with him — I just didn't know why.

I sat there looking at the words and looking around me for answers. I felt like I had the answers and the questions, I just needed to *connect* them. I was trapped between a feeling of excitement and puzzlement. I wanted to find an outlet to the energy inside me. I wanted to shout!

This time, when he explained emotions to me, I didn't get the feeling that I understood. I didn't feel any rush of adrenalin. I knew this new statement was important. Of course, I wrote it down but it didn't feel like my mind was on a rocket racing up into space. I just felt more *puzzled* than anything.

My second meeting with the Magician had filled me with doubt. It seemed to drift into my mind like a gentle breeze. Maybe he didn't deserve the title I'd given him. How can you propose to explain the human mind in one sentence, or two, or even ten for that matter? What does that mean anyway that "emotion is the mind's way of telling you that there's been a change in certainty"? I felt uncertain. More uncertain than earlier that day, actually. I felt a little beaten. I desperately needed to make sense of these words. But was comprehension within my grasp, or was it disappearing like my friend into the distance whistling as it escaped from my mind?

I no longer felt like sitting at the top of the hill. The wind was out of my sails. I no longer felt like I would find the answers to my puzzle up here. All I'd written was the two statements he'd told me. Not much compared to the previous night's book-writing exercise.

My enthusiasm had tapered off and I needed a change in venue. I decided to head down to the bar from last night which I discovered was called the *Out-o-Kilter* and take a look at the lunch menu. The food had looked good the previous night and I knew I'd feel comfortable there.

Maybe some high cholesterol food and a good beer would give me the energy to focus on my thoughts. What am I saying? Of course it would! Who doesn't love a good pub lunch? I relinquished my position on the rock as if it was an acknowledgement of defeat. No, I had to be positive. Understanding had to be ahead of me. I just needed to be positive.

As I walked down the hill, I tried beating this new idea into my mind through repetition:

"All emotions are created by a change in certainty."

I repeated it over and over, in time with my step. I even added it to imaginary rock n' roll solos, as if that might help. And somehow I think that helped boost my spirit. Maybe it was the silliness of my behavior, but as I marched into town I felt more at peace; as if I'd accepted that everything would be as it should and the answer would arrive in my mind when it was ready.

And it was with a relaxed and patient air that I spent the rest of the day. The wheels were turning within my mind. I was a new man. I was changing, growing, deepening; I just didn't know where I would end up with these new ideas.

That night I lay in bed thinking about my time in Edinburgh, and I couldn't help but marvel at the beauty of life. I'd been in such a deep slump; my winter of discontent so to speak. But now I felt at one with life. I'd regained my stability and happiness all at once. What mystical trickery was at work within my life?

With my eyes closed, I started to give in to sleep. I recalled fragments of fragments of the dreams from previous nights. What was that image I saw in my mind? Where had my dreams taken me lately? Was I dreaming more over the last few days or was it just that I could remember more of my dreams?

Hard as it was to focus on detail, I felt like there were reflections within my dreams of what I was experiencing while awake. I wondered what the meaning of dreams might be. Was that the last thing I thought about before falling asleep, or the last thing I now remember? It didn't matter really, I was asleep, free from the strictures that define consciousness.

Chapter IV

The Congregation

*T*he grand doors at the front of the Opera House are open and as the crowds of people bustle into the main theatre for this evening's grand magic show, the Engineer sits in his assigned seat, soaking in the ambience.

There is something unique about the live performances; something that distinguishes them from the movies that are also shown here. They are more intense, more consuming, and more deeply based in reality, with their own sense of individuality.

The first thing he noticed when he walked into the theater earlier was the strange smell in the air; a fusion of many different fragrances combining together into something special. At first, he could smell people's perfumes, and the aroma of food and drink had also crept in from the large buffet that was set up outside the main theatre in the central lobby, but as he entered the main auditorium, the smell evolved. As he took in this new space, the scent in the air became more humid, smoky, even musty.

He could see some of the audience members smoking from old-fashioned pipes, as was allowed prior to the show. Large, free-standing candle arbors held clusters of tall candlesticks, emitting their own, smoky aroma as the wax was consumed by each flame.

As he moved to his seat, he noted the old leather-covered seats and beautifully ornate hardwood frames. Even these added something particular and unique to the smell. As he sat down, he took in a deep breath, relaxing, relishing his time in the theatre as if it were his first.

Comfortable now, he studied his surroundings more closely, gazing up at the lighting up above. What was different about it? There was a great chandelier in the center of the ceiling elevated high above the audience, with smaller chandeliers equally spaced around the auditorium. These were also large, but when situated so closely to the great chandelier they seemed small by comparison. The Engineer knew this was just a visual illusion; these were precisely the details he appreciated.

Besides the chandeliers, there were many smaller lamps around the theatre, not to mention the large stage lights that were being systematically tested by their operators as they readied for the show. Above the various lighting, the elevated ceiling looked far-away — even from his seat in the raised second tier known as the Pavilion.

As the audience funneled into their designated seats, there was a musical ebb and flow in the conversations amongst various parties of excited patrons, the laughter and volume of their voices giving hint to their own nervousness before the evening's performance.

Not only that, but as the gaggle of people passed by the Engineer, he enjoyed gazing at all the different dresses and formal attire that they'd chosen; the bright colors, the beautiful though sometimes gaudy designs, as well as the matching outfits of some couples.

As he politely greeted the new arrivals that were fortunate enough to sit in his area, he noted that some of their faces were familiar. They were obviously regulars, as he would certainly not know them from his introverted social life. Yet he recognized their faces as well as the glow of excitement that most of them seemed to share. This was clearly a special night for many of the patrons.

Every show the Engineer came to was unique, both on stage and off. Each performance was different but not always dissimilar. There was a grand design behind each performance but also a refreshing randomness that only added to the beauty of the event. He came to every performance as was his luxury, as was his pleasure … as was his vice.

He could not say what it was that drew him to these shows. It was something instinctive that he struggled to understand, though he would ponder the meaning of his addiction to this simple pleasure on a regular basis. While he could make every sense of the mechanical aspects, it wasn't within his skill set to understand the mental aspects of his life.

Of course, there must be a pattern of some type, but it was just something that eluded him at that time. That was his belief anyway. Maybe that was the beauty of the experience — meaning lost in complexity, woven or crafted so carefully that he was unable to define its significance.

What was difficult to determine was why his experiences in the theatre were so different from his real life. Was it just that he felt his senses were overwhelmed by the activity of it all? Was it just too busy and intricate for his mind to process? Or maybe the excitement of the coming show was influencing his interpretation of his environment. It was unclear to him exactly why these events were so special, which only enhanced the grand mystery of it all, which is why he came to enjoy these performances.

As the last of the audience settled into their seats, the lights began to dim, candles were snuffed out, and the electric lamps were dimmed until they could not be seen. As if a secret signal had been passed through the audience, a hushed silence came over the entire auditorium. A lone cough echoed briefly through the space, but all the patrons looked politely, intently, toward the stage in respectful silence. Finally, there was complete darkness. The show was about to start.

Chapter 5

Logic and Poetry

*T*he following morning I found it difficult to pull myself out of sleep. Each time my alarm went off, I hit the snooze button and drifted effortlessly back into slumber. I would then be drawn back into my dreams, only to be pulled awake by the alarm clock once more.

My mind struggled to recall the previous evening. I couldn't remember going to sleep, which I didn't mind too much. So often we wake up in the morning ignorant of the change that occurred between wakefulness and slumber, almost as though our mind doesn't consider the transition important enough to recall.

The first thing we experience when falling asleep, I've thought to myself more than once, is the loss of consciousness. If the first step of sleep is to lose consciousness, why would we have any memory of the experience at all? Maybe when the lights go off, so also does the metaphorical video recorder.

At the same time, we occasionally seem to remember fragments of our dreams. I say "we" remember, but I really mean our conscious mind remembers. Somehow, as we are waking and we sever the connection with sleep, we catch a glimpse of the dreams — the whisper of a memory — that had been entertaining us while our mind drifted in unconscious bliss.

Much like when you're at the movies and as you walk towards the theater that is playing your movie, you hear snippets from the theater next door. For a brief moment, you might try to guess which movie is playing, or maybe the scene, and you struggle to identify it. And then, you arrive at your theater and your previous thoughts are abandoned as the excitement of your coming experience overtakes your senses.

Why is it so difficult to hold onto the memories of our dreams? It seems that if we stop thinking about them for even a second, they seem to vanish from our consciousness, escaping back to where they wish to reside somewhere behind the intangible vale that separates us from our subconscious mind. Maybe they're not our memories to keep. Maybe that movie experience is only for the people in the cinema next door.

Eventually, I got myself organized and stepped out of my hotel room with a spring in my step. As I left the hotel and headed out for a meal at what had become my Edinburgh "Local" I realized that I'd just about given up trying to figure out the meaning in the Magician's words …. At least I'd accepted that I wasn't going to figure it all out before lunch.

Once again, when I arrived at the pub I searched for a cozy table where I could enjoy my lunch and reflect on my life in peace. As I looked around from the entrance, I spotted Rob, my amiable barman, who was reading a book and looked "off duty." Happy to see him, I waved and said hello as he looked over.

"Hi, James!" he greeted me in his friendly way. "Alright?" he asked, in a genuine manner.

"I'm good, thanks. Are you working today?" I asked, as I walked over to his table.

"No, just dropped in for a bite to eat and to pick up my pay check. Are you here to write your second novel?" he asked, the hint of a smirk dancing across his face.

"No, no," I chuckled. "Thought I'd check out the lunch menu."

He invited me to join him and recommended some items from the menu; nothing low-cal of course. I'd enjoyed his conversation from the other night so decided to accept the invitation. I felt more comfortable joining him than eating at a separate table, especially now that I knew he was there to eat, not to work.

"Thanks, that sounds good," I said as I sat down and proceeded to order a beer and some food from the barmaid that came to the table.

"So, what brings you to Edinburgh?" asked Rob.

"Well, I'm not sure," I answered honestly. "I was invited by a friend who's here for work who suggested I come up and take some time off from London."

"And how do you like it?" he probed.

"I love it. I love Edinburgh and it's turned out to be an amazing holiday; life-changing even. You never know what life is going to throw at you!" I said with a snort.

"Really? Ah, it's a great town," he offered in acknowledgement.

"So, did you meet one of the local lasses?" he asked.

"No," I said, twisting my head in confused surprise, trying to understand the question. "Oh, you're referring to the 'life-changing' bit. No, I mean, yeah, I met some of the locals — but that's not what I meant." And I shook my head, wondering what I really meant.

I didn't feel like sharing my story. I wanted to, of course. I wanted to tell my friends and family that everything was different now. I wanted to explain why. I just didn't know how. I didn't know *how* I could explain my experience, or if anyone would understand.

I met a weird, mysterious man on a hill who somehow fixed me by telling me two statements that made no sense. How could I expect anyone to understand something like that?

"Well, I'm glad that Edinburgh has been so special for you," Rob offered, as I wasn't forthcoming in my thoughts. "You know, there's something about getting away from work and the big city that allows people to get perspective. Sometimes we can't understand what's missing from our lives without getting away from our lives."

He paused momentarily before asking, "You want to hear something funny? A lot of people that I meet here have interesting experiences while in Edinburgh," and he paused while trying to find the right word. "I don't know why, but they seem to be in a different place when they leave here than when they arrive. Do you know what I mean?" he asked genuinely.

I nodded out of politeness, not knowing whether I wanted to share my thoughts. I didn't want to give away what I really thought. I was on the brink of sharing my experiences with my friend the barman. I liked Rob; he had a very affable way about him. It must be an interesting insight into people's worlds, being a barman, learning about them as they enter your world briefly.

"You must meet all sorts of people here, don't you?" I asked.

"Yeah, it's fascinating, coming to work each day. Every day, I meet a different bunch, you know. I enjoy talking to people. Learning about them. I try to have a positive influence on them. As much as I can, anyway. People come here for all sorts of reasons and with a variety of different mindsets. I'd like it if they leave my bar happier than when they arrive." He shrugged as he said this.

The food arrived and while we ate I contemplated the idea of getting his thoughts on my experiences over the last two days. Was my experience something I could share? Why did I feel so comfortable talking with Rob? I wondered how I could get his opinion without entering into a conversation I wasn't ready for. Why would he understand what I was going through? As I accepted defeat by my food and pushed my lunch away from me in acknowledgement, I thought of a way that I could speak without giving away too much.

"Let me ask you something, Rob," I said, pausing to allow the barmaid on duty to take our plates away. "I met this character a couple of days ago," I shook my head trying to figure out how to explain myself.

"He was a magician," I said, blurting it out

"Like a street performer?" Rob suggested, nodding away

"Well, yeah, like a street performer," I accepted, thinking that was the best way to keep things simple.

"Okay, we have a lot of street entertainers. Yeah, some

of them are interesting guys. I've met a few of them. Maybe I know the one you mean?" he suggested. I guess he must get to know a lot of the local performers both as patrons of the bar as well as acquaintances on the street. But now the conversation was leading us in the wrong direction.

"No, I don't think you know this guy," I said, with a degree of confidence that made Rob give me a quizzical look. How did I know that he didn't know this guy?

"Anyway," I said, trying to keep focused, "He performed a magic trick and I'm trying to figure out how he did it."

And now I was lost. How do I ask him about magic without describing the trick that was performed?

"I saw a guy do this trick and I can't figure out how he did it," I repeated.

"In fact, I can't seem to get it out of my mind. Do you have any idea how they fool us?" I asked. "How do magicians, these guys that perform in the squares, trick us? I can't figure it out," I asked, hoping that I'd kept things simple, straight forward, and as deliberately vague as possible.

"You mean, how does magic work?" he asked quizzically. I nodded, trying to hide my awkwardness at asking such a weird question.

"You know, you're an engineer, right? You said engineers work things out. You look at a puzzle and you figure it out. How do people trick us with magic?" I asked, trying to lend a degree of context to my question.

"Well, for starters," he began, "I don't think we're meant to understand. That's the point!" he said, pausing to think.

"You're right though," he admitted. "Magic is like any puzzle, only they make you think the puzzle is going to turn out as one thing and then it turns out to be something completely different," he said, offering open hands to see if that was what I was asking.

"When I think of magic," he continued, "I think of a guy in a fancy suit hiding an item from the audience and somehow transforming it into a bouquet of flowers or a bunch of white doves. The real magic is to convince the audience that one thing is going to happen and then present them with a different outcome that would appear impossible," he said, "Is that what you're asking?"

"Ah, not really," I said. "Don't get me wrong. I like how you explain it. I was just trying to understand the mechanics of it."

"Well," he said, "the magician has to combine a number of practiced steps that, when separate, don't necessarily appear as magic but when combined, correctly produce a spectacle that your mind can't believe possible. We, therefore, accept magic as the method of creating this seemingly impossible spectacle. Each step has to be clever in itself. Each step involves skills, techniques or props that allow the magician to carry out a step that would not normally be apparent to the audience. If you can combine these steps in a clever manner such that it appears impossible, you can confuse the audience sufficiently to convince them that it was magic."

I nodded to Rob. Obviously, his explanation seemed logical. But it didn't really help. I needed it to be clearer. And to do that, I needed to tell him more. While I was sure that I would be entering into a conversation that would make no sense and end in embarrassment, I decided that I needed to share with Rob my story from the last two days. Maybe there was less risk of embarrassment with a relative stranger that I would not see again after I left Edinburgh. My friends and family may view my story as odd, which I would have to live with every time I saw them.

So I told him my story. I tried to keep it simple, if that's possible given the context, but I had no idea how Rob would react to hearing my story. You have to admit it is a bit out there. So I jumped into the deep end and hoped for the best:

"Rob, I've been trying to keep things simple because I don't know how to explain what I've been through in the last couple days. I'd like to ask your opinion, I just don't know how to explain myself," I said, pausing. He looked at me thoughtfully and asked:

"Is this about the puzzle that you were writing about last night?" he asked.

"Yeah," I nodded. "I'd like to share my experience, but I just don't know if you have the time or whether you're interested."

"I'll tell you what," he said, looking at his watch. "It's my day off so if you buy the beers I'll have both the time and the interest!" he said smiling.

"I'll buy you lunch as well if you can riddle me this puzzle," I said, chuckling.

"Done!" he said quickly, accepting the terms of our social contract before I could decide whether I was joking or not. We ordered another round and I started recounting my meeting on the hill.

"Now, you have to understand this is not the story you're expecting. And it is a little weird. However, yesterday I met a stranger up on the hillside over there and somehow he reached inside my head and tore out all my negativity and replaced it with positivity. Right?" I said, pausing for a sip of beer and looking to see his reaction.

"You seemed to be pretty excited last night when you came to the bar," he said, nodding.

"Right. But, that's not me. I mean, I've been in a slump for a long time. I came up here to Edinburgh to escape my life and figure out what was wrong with it. Rather, what was wrong with me. And somehow, without me knowing how, this guy on the hill was able to literally change how I thought."

"Somehow," I continued, "he just kind of fixed my mind. Just like that. It was the briefest of conversations. But by the end of it, I was a different person. And I don't know how he did it. That's why I was calling him a magician. How can someone do that if it's not magic?" I asked.

While I was excited to share my story, I was also aware that it may not be the kind of conversation that other people would entertain.

"Okay, so, what did he say?" asked Rob, still appearing to be genuinely interested as he lent back in his chair and focused on what I was saying.

I grabbed my pad and turned to the page where I'd written the two statements that I thought were the key to understanding what he said and slid it across the table for Rob to read.

"He said a number of things, but this is what seemed to be the key. He said that these statements explain my thoughts as well as my emotions. And it was when I heard the first statement that something seemed to change in me. I don't know if there was something in the words or whether it was something about the man on the hill. I can't explain it."

He looked at the words on the page:

"All actions are taken to increase certainty."

&

"All emotions are created by a change in certainty."

After a few moments, he looked back at me and this was probably when I felt most nervous. I guess I was wondering whether he was going to think I was crazy or not. Was he about to burst into laughter, as some people might? But he looked at me and with the same honest and caring manner asked, "So, this is it?"

"He said these words and you think he did something to your mind?" he asked.

I could not tell how serious he was taking the conversation but I responded, "Yes! And I don't *think* he did something to my mind, I know he did."

"Like I say," I continued, "I don't understand it. He said that these two statements explain how my mind works and I believe him. How can two statements explain the entirety of my mind? It's crazy! But somehow I feel that he is right. I don't know why, I can't explain it. I just feel it. Every time I read the words, they make me more certain that they are true. What do you think? I mean I know what you're going to say, this guy is crazy, or maybe I'm crazy, but, there's something there, I know it," I said earnestly.

"Well," he said slowly, perhaps pausing to find something positive to say but looking a little doubtful, "there are certainly laws that govern aspects of science. You know, statements that can be applied in physics that explain how aspects of our environment behave. Like Newton's Laws of Motion for example," he offered, pausing to see if I knew what he meant.

"But," he continued, "I've never heard of anyone trying to explain the human mind in terms of statements that explain our thoughts and emotions. There are no laws that govern human thought. We are all just who we are; we all just think what we think."

He paused while mulling over the concept. It looked like he was undecided about the possibility.

"I don't believe that you can explain human behavior or how the mind works in a couple of statements," he said. "That doesn't make sense to me either. But I do think that every puzzle is a challenge. The question I have is: how is it that these words have had such an influence on you?" he asked rhetorically.

"I don't know," I said. "That's what's confounding me."

"I'll tell you what," he said, "you leave me with this overnight and I bet you by tomorrow I can tell you something that will help. I can't say I can explain it all, as this is not the type of puzzle I'm used to, but I can give it a try. How does that sound?"

"Okay," I readily agreed. "Maybe we can meet here again tomorrow and I'll buy you lunch again?" I offered.

"Why don't you reserve that offer until you see what I come up with?" he proposed.

"Okay, deal!" I said. I settled up the tab, said "Cheerio" and made my way back into the wind-chilled weather outside.

I decided to take a walk around town. Most of the people that I saw on the streets seemed to be working or on their way to work. Of course, you could spot the tourists a mile away: holding a map; looking in opposite directions alternately; some with oversized backpacks, others with clothing that somehow looked American. There were plenty of tourists. Just like me I guess.

I wondered what my "tourist" telltales were? I looked at myself in the reflection of a shop window. I wasn't lost like the other tourists. I was found! I just didn't know where I was going. I don't know what my clothing indicated, but the look in my eyes said *I know where I am.* Well, that's what it felt like anyway. I smiled at my reflection and went on my way again.

So I had found myself. I'd found myself in Edinburgh. What did that mean? I hadn't worked that side of things out yet. All I knew was that I wasn't lost any more. My life wasn't hopeless; it had meaning again.

What had Rob said about magic? He'd said that each step involved in the magic trick had to be clever in itself but when combined, produce a result that was inexplicable. So how had the Magician done that to my mind? I couldn't see how a stranger could assemble a magic trick within someone else's mind without them knowing about it. But isn't that how we experience all magic? As a juxtaposition of conflicting beliefs about what should and shouldn't be possible.

Of course, there are times when people or events can change our emotional state from happiness to sadness or vice-versa. But that's not magic. Maybe you're watching a movie or listening to music when you feel your emotional states shift between fear and relief or compassion to joy. But the magic that I'd experienced wasn't as simple as an emotional shift; it was more like a shift in how my mind interpreted life. Like the wiring within my mind had been changed. Like he'd taken out the bad circuitry and replaced it with a modernized, upgraded version.

I pictured the Magician sitting on the rock, staring into my soul. His magic trick started from a belief by me that there was nothing that could pull me out of my hole. After years of aimless stagnancy I'd accepted that I was lost. My mind was defeated and I was entirely sure that nothing and no one could help me or save me. But he took me from a place of hopelessness to a place of hope and positivity when I was adamant that I was lost. That was real magic.

But if I could understand how he did it, would it still be magic? I remember when I was at school and the science teacher would first of all show us an experiment we'd never seen before and everyone's interest would be tweaked as some miracle of science occurred.

Then he'd demonstrate the science behind this new idea he was trying to teach. It wasn't magic, it was *science*. There was a logical explanation that we all now understood. The magic was gone, replaced by logic. Was this the same? Would I still respect the magic if I could explain it?

The magic only works if the audience can't comprehend how the trick is possible. So how does anyone reach into your mind and "fix" it without you understanding how? That's what I was asking myself as I wandered through the streets.

When I try to remember the events of that day, I can't remember exactly what I did for the rest of the afternoon or evening. I guess that means I didn't get up too much. I may have met up with Simon for dinner or drinks. I only remember that I was *happy*. Life was good. When I look back now, life has been good ever since. I'm not saying that bad things haven't happened. I've probably had to deal with more pain and heartbreak than I'd experienced back then.

It's just that ever since my trip to Edinburgh, I've looked at life through different eyes and, like the barman and his positive outlook on life, I try and make the best out of whatever experiences life sends my way.

So another intriguing day ended and the only thing I regret now is not writing down more of my thoughts from back then. People use the term "enlightened" in respect to religion, but that's how my experiences made me feel. With each day, I felt more enlightened. That may sound over-the-top, but maybe what I experienced was actually a kind of spiritual awakening.

After another day of excitement and intrigue, I lay in my bed pondering all the new ideas that had recently populated my mind. How do we calm our minds when they are overtaken by excitement? How do we fall asleep when our minds remain so active? That night, I felt like a kid on Christmas Eve, enveloped in the mystery of tomorrow's gifts.

Every thought that entered my mind only added to the fever pitch of excitement that I was now experiencing. Yet somehow, as we all do, I eventually drifted into sleep. As my mind was wandering along some path I cannot recall, an unseen switch was flicked.

As my thoughts clouded with ideas that I could not yet clarify into distinction, my mind managed to take control and separate me from myself. For the next few hours, my thoughts were on holidays, travelling where they pleased — free to roam, without me to guide them.

I was asleep.

Chapter V

*A*s the Engineer sat in the darkness, waiting in anticipation for the evening's performance to commence, he felt rather than heard a deep rumble as a lone drumbeat started ever-so-softly at a rapid rate. The soft vibration grew louder, into the clear sound of deep drums as a second drummer joined the first.

As the sound increased in volume, more drummers joined in, progressively adding to the palpable energy that filled the theatre until it finally reached a deafening volume. All at once, the drums ceased and the stage lights came on, illuminating a lone figure on center stage. The crowd all gave him a generous round of applause. This was who they had come to see.

The man stood at the front of the stage regarding the audience with an intent expression. He looked over the crowd with the appearance of supreme confidence. He didn't speak;

he just gazed outward, as if searching for specific individuals.

His clothes were simple, yet formal; a black evening suit of typical cut, with a grey shirt underneath. His shoes, black polished leather. His bow-tie and gloves were matching silver. He wore a long, black cape over the suit, with silver trim along the edges.

And finally, there was his hat. It was the fashion those days for all magicians to wear a top hat. His was black, though quite weathered around the edges and crumpled in places, as if it may have been crushed at some point. It wasn't quite cylindrical in shape, as it was wider in circumference at top than bottom, with the lower brim curled upward on each side. There was a slightly comical look about it, as was his fancy.

He held his gaze upon the crowd until he was sure that it had been too long for their own comfort. He could sense a nervous tension coming from the crowd. Right from the beginning, he needed to make sure that they knew that what was about to happen next wasn't what they expected, and that he alone was in charge of tonight's proceedings. He was their host and they were his audience. He was the conductor and they were his orchestra.

"Good evening, Madams and Messieurs," he announced with a flourish. "It is my privilege and honor to be here tonight to host this evening's entertainment." He paused briefly, taking in the moment.

"I am sure you have all come to see magic, have you not? But, I ask you now, what is magic?" he said, pausing again while looking at the audience questioningly.

"Tonight, I shall dazzle your senses with acts that defy logic. I shall make you question your own sense about what is real and what is possible as I give you the impossible."

The audience, mesmerized, hung on his every word.

"I ask you now, how can something that is impossible be possible?" he continued. "That is the beauty of magic. That is what I shall give you tonight. These are no cheap tricks for children's parties. Hear me when I tell you that it doesn't matter whether you believe in magic or not. Because when you leave here tonight, I know that each and every one of you will believe that *anything* is possible."

"Now, who would like to see some magic?" he asked, opening his arms in an inviting gesture.

The audience broke out into applause once more and the Magician moved towards the back of the stage to prepare for his first act.

The Engineer sat straight in his seat, relishing the evening's performance even more than usual. His seat was only a few rows back, in the center of the second tier. It was a fine location to see every aspect of the show. As he watched the Magician set up the stage, he pondered the words of the Magician.

How can something that is impossible be possible? What a wonderful proposition, he thought. As he looked around the audience, he could see that every person had their eyes focused keenly on the stage. The Magician owned the audience. They were transfixed by his every movement.

The Magician was now starting his first magic trick. A table had been placed next to him by his female assistant and as he stood inspecting it, he lifted the table and moved it to a new location. In the meantime, the assistant had returned with an empty birdcage, which she handed to the Magician. He inspected it carefully, turning it upside down, opening the cage door, and finally, with a nod of approval, he placed it on the table.

Next, the assistant returned with three white doves. She handed them, one by one, to the Magician and as they attempted to flutter away he placed them inside the birdcage. Once all three were placed inside, he closed and locked the door in place behind them.

The assistant also carried three sharp knives which she handed to the Magician one at a time. As his eyes glanced between the knives in hand and the doves in the cage he looked at the assistant quizzically. The audience chuckled nervously at his mock confusion.

His finger then went up, as if in sudden realization. He handed the knives back to the assistant one by one and then proceeded to remove his cape and place it over the birdcage, apparently protecting the birds from the terrible possibility of a hapless fate.

As he stood there, he looked as if to ponder what should happen next. And then, in one swift movement he began to inflate a balloon. It was a large, white balloon with silver stars, almost perfectly spherical in shape.

Once inflated, he walked over to the table and rubbed the balloon on his cape, which was now resting on the birdcage. He then let go of the balloon, as if to inspect it, but for some reason it wasn't to his satisfaction. So he placed the balloon on his cape once more and rubbed it backwards and forwards, but more aggressively this time.

After a quick re-inspection, it was clear that he was happy with the balloon and he released it, sending it floating up into the air high above the crowd. It drifted aimlessly through the air, carried in random directions by unseen currents.

Now that the crowd was aware of what he was doing, he rapidly carried out the same process with two more balloons, sending them floating off over the audience. The balloons were each lit up with spotlights as they drifted around the large auditorium, the silver stars illuminating the theater in all directions. By the time the last one was floating above the crowd, the first balloon had come within reach of a patron, who pushed it back into the air with delight.

At last, the Magician was ready.

As the assistant handed the knives back to him once more, a drum roll commenced. The Magician faced the audience with knives in hand, looking at each balloon intently. Then with a suddenness of movement that one would not expect for a man of his age, he flung the first knife above the crowd at the first balloon.

There was a scream from one or two patrons. As the knife hit the balloon, a loud clash of cymbals was heard, and a large puff of smoke exploded from the balloon at the same time a white dove was released from it. The crowd cheered and applauded.

As the Magician focused on the next balloon, the drum roll recommenced, and with the clash of cymbals and a puff of smoke, the second white dove flew to its freedom. The audience was now standing and applauding as he threw the last knife and released the last of the doves. Strangely enough, the knives had not fallen down into the audience after each balloon burst.

As the crowd applauded, the Magician walked over to the table and collected his cape, settling it around his suit. But in so doing he allowed the audience to see the cage that was now empty but for the three knives. The Magician feigned a look of mock surprise as he removed the knives and presented them to the audience.

Now, the Magician could see that everyone in the auditorium was standing and applauding. As he and his assistant joined each other center stage to bow in gratitude to the audience, the Magician saw the face in the crowd.

The first time when he bowed, he was uncertain. But, after a second glance he was sure that he recognized the man standing up in the second tier, near the front right in the middle.

The Magician smiled to himself as he knew that tonight was going to be special. No longer would the stranger in the audience be a mystery to him. This peculiar ignorance had gone on long enough. Tonight, the Magician had decided to weave this individual into his plans. He now shifted his attention to the next magic trick as the orchestra played some fun, uplifting tune to provide time for preparations to be completed for the next trick.

The Engineer sat down once more after enjoying the first magic trick. He was elated, mystified. How could the Magician make that which was impossible — possible? For if he was to believe his eyes, then he'd just witnessed the impossible.

But as he sat there watching the stage even more keenly, he had the uncomfortable feeling that the Magician had just looked directly at him. It had happened before, but this time it appeared that the Magician had looked straight at the Engineer with a curious or even dangerous smile. What could such familiarity mean?

The rest of the first act was a rollercoaster of emotions as the crowd went from doubt to fear, surprise to relief, satisfaction to curiosity. The magic tricks were all a combination of traditional ideas, but always with an unexpected twist. And when it came to his miraculous tricks, the Magician did not disappoint.

There were rabbits disappearing and reappearing, as if from thin air. Stainless steel rings that somehow were looped together only to be separated while the Magician juggled them. At one point, it appeared that the Magician was even able to levitate half a foot off the stage through the power of his own mind.

In the final trick of the first act, the Magician was able to cut the assistant in half while in a box and even had the bottom half walk around on-stage, as if looking for its top half — a most disturbing image until the two halves were miraculously reconnected and the crowd could see that the assistant was unharmed.

After another round of excited applause, the stage curtains were closed as the Magician and his assistant bowed courteously to the audience. The orchestra began playing peaceful music and the lights around the theatre came back on.

It was time for intermission.

Chapter 6

A Spectrum of Color

*T*he following morning, when I caught up with Simon for breakfast, it was clear to him that something was different. He could see the change in my demeanor, from my walk to how I said "good morning," and he commented on this as we sipped on our coffees.

"What's going on, man?" he quizzed me.

"What do you mean?" I smiled back in response.

"You've been acting differently over the last couple of days. Did you meet a girl? What have you been up to and why don't I know all the details?" he asked.

"No, no romance or one-night stands, for that matter," I said, a little cagey about my new perspective on life and letting a little pride sneak into my attitude.

"Well, what's going on?" Simon pushed. "You're like, radiating some kind of positive aura that I've never seen before in you. I told you that a trip would do you good, but I hardly recognize you. You haven't been recruited by some religious cult or something, have you? Or, maybe someone has been giving you happy pills?"

"No," I answered with a laugh, "I just got myself sorted out."

Simon rubbed his hands over his face, trying to understand what was going on.

"Really? Don't get me wrong, I'm happy for you," he said, "I just don't know who this new James is that's sitting before me. What did you do with the real James?" he asked, looking into my eyes in a comical manner.

"It's me, Simon," I answered. "I *am* the real James. I just feel different. I'm happy. It's like the storm is finally over," I answered honestly, looking at him sincerely.

He looked at me, nodding his head, as if to say, "Too right!"

"Well, that's wonderful news. I told you to get away from London for a bit, I told you! And here you're all high on life. Was I right or was I right?" he asked happily, clapping his hands together, apparently taking some credit for my newfound happiness.

"We need to celebrate. I have a lot on at work today, but let's meet after I finish and wrap up this trip with a big night out, Edinburgh style!" he said.

"Alright, sounds like a plan," I said, accepting his idea with enthusiasm, even though I was already exhausted from the last few days.

A celebration was definitely in order. After seeing Edinburgh nightlife during the week, I was sure the weekend would be a real party.

But as much as he continued to probe me over breakfast for an explanation to this happiness that my time in Edinburgh had awoken, I maintained that I'd just had a nice time and that a break from London was apparently all I needed.

I knew he didn't believe my cover story, but it was all that I was prepared to offer at that stage. For some reason, I felt more relaxed speaking to Rob, who I'd just met, about my experience rather than to Simon, whom I'd known for years. It was odd, but I was quite sure that I wasn't ready to talk to him yet about the changes I was going through.

"Enough, Simon!" I said, raising my hands in the air, "I'll tell you about it another time!" I said, hoping to finish the conversation.

So we parted ways and I filled in time browsing through shops, waiting for my lunch rendezvous with Rob-the-barman at my local. I wasn't expecting too much from him. I was excited to find out what he had to say, but I wasn't expecting him to understand what I'd experienced or what the words meant.

Why should he be in a better position to understand my mind than me? After all, he was an engineer — not a psychologist! I filled in time distracting myself in and amongst the local shops and markets. There was always something happening around town.

Today, there was a market with all sorts of colorful artwork carefully placed on easels and presented by the local artists. Each stall had something different ranging from paintings to clay sculptures, and strange metal men that had been welded together with left-over scrap metal. I wasn't there to shop, but it kept me distracted all the same.

When I arrived at the bar, it was just opening and still fairly empty. I saw no sign of Rob and set myself up in a corner with my back to the wall, facing the rest of the bar.

There's something so warm and inviting about the bars in Edinburgh. I'd noticed the same thing in London. I don't know whether it's the contrast in temperature between inside and outside, the burning flames in the fireplace, the warm lighting coming from antique chandeliers contrasted to the dreary weather outside or maybe the Brits simply know how to do warm, cozy bars well! In any case, I felt relaxed and content, sitting there sipping on a beer while I waited for Rob.

I took my pad out and was idly skimming through my scribblings, not really focusing on them, when I saw him bustle in, shaking off the cold as he stepped inside. He spotted me straight away and, after a quick word with the barman on duty, headed over with a look of satisfaction.

We exchanged greetings as he unwrapped himself from his scarf and jacket. I asked him with some excitement whether he'd had a chance to think about what we'd discussed the previous day.

"I did!" he said with an intriguing smile.

"I don't know whether this is the explanation you were looking for," he said, as be placed a notepad of his own on the table. "But I think I've figured out the two statements that your friend on the hill gave you."

"Really?" I said, openly surprised, not sure whether I could believe my good fortune and eager to hear everything.

"I can't be sure that I'm on the right track but, well, last night I was scratching my head trying to nut it out when I had a 'Eureka' moment and step by step, it all came together. There's still plenty of work to do, but I think between the two of us we can make sense of it," he said expectantly.

His eyes showed excitement. It was a look that I hadn't seen from Rob. He clearly believed he was on the right track and was looking to confirm it with me. He was noticeably absorbed in the challenge we set forth the previous day.

The other barman brought over a couple drinks while Rob got himself organized and we both took a sip of our drinks, as if preparing ourselves for the challenge ahead. It felt like we were attempting to translate some ancient Egyptian text that we'd just discovered, which was odd considering the text was just two, simple sentences ... in English.

"So," he said, in a focused and enthusiastic manner. "I was looking at the first statement for some time last night, trying to figure out how to break it down as I would any engineering system."

Rob leaned forward, clearly excited about sharing his thoughts.

"And I decided that there is some information inherent in the statement that is not stated. I mean, to understand the statement we have to ask what the statement is in reference to," Rob explained.

"If, as your friend on the hill suggested, these statements explain how your mind works, then we have to refer all meaning to the mind. Any mind. That is, we have to look at the words from the perspective of the mind. Are you with me so far?" he asked as he paused to take a sip of his drink.

"Makes sense. But how does that help?" I asked, not really understanding his point.

"Well, let's look at the statement," and he wrote the first statement on a fresh sheet of paper:

All actions are taken to increase certainty.

"I was staring at the word *certainty* last night when I asked the question: certainty of what? We use 'certainty' in a number of different ways," he said.

"It may be in reference to our certainty of the past, present or future. It may be regarding our certainty in our self or in our understanding of our environment. But regardless of how we are using the term, it is always ultimately relative to ourselves. And that's when it started to make sense. First of all, he is talking about the certainty of the mind. Secondly, he's talking about the certainty of the mind within in the context of a given environment."

"Doesn't certainty just mean how sure you're of something?" I asked.

"Of course, but ultimately we are expressing certainty, or a degree of certainty, of information that is relevant and relative to us given our current situation. That is, the mind is evaluating a degree of certainty regarding self within a particular environment. It could be relevant to aspects of our past, present or future. But in every case, it is used in the context of self within a given environment. Did I explain that correctly?" he asked, with a quizzical smile.

"I'm not sure. But I wouldn't mind if you explain it again." I said, uncertain of the meaning of his words.

"Well, what if he's using these statements purely in the mathematical sense? What if the idea is that these statements are axioms that we can use to interpret our emotions or choose our actions?" he asked.

"I'm sorry, what do you mean by 'axiom'?" I interjected, with a look of open ignorance.

"Well, an axiom is like a rule that we accept as true. Like

a mathematical equation that we can use to define aspects of life," Rob explained patiently.

"If we accept that certainty is of 'self,' that the statement is in the context of a given 'environment,' and that 'action' is any choice that the mind makes, then the first statement is basically saying that all choices that we make are for the purpose of improving stability of self within a particular situation. It sounds simple, but I guess that's the point." He paused, sipping on his beer before continuing.

"I think he's saying that the purpose of the mind is to increase the certainty of itself within its environment." And he paused to allow me to respond to this idea.

"It sounds a bit obvious, doesn't it? Of course we all take actions to help us survive. I asked him that when I met him the second time. 'If you're hungry — you eat. If you're thirsty — you drink,' I said to him. I don't think there's anything unusual in that." I shrugged and felt a little disappointed in where our conversation was going.

"No," he said, still beaming with enthusiasm. "That's not it. I mean, that's a part of it, but listen to this," Rob said, setting it up.

"When we think of an action we think of physical things we do like jumping out of the way of a car or running to the train as it pulls into the platform. Remember, he's talking about your mind. He said these statements explain your mind. That means that when he refers to actions, he's talking about what actions you take inside your mind just as much as our physical actions."

He paused, looking at me, before continuing to drain his beer.

"He's saying, or at least I think he's saying, that the purpose of every thought is to increase certainty of self relative to the environment. I say 'self' as I'm still unsure whether he's meaning just the mind or whether that includes the rest of the human body. But I don't think it matters for our purposes. The important thing to understand is that he is proposing that any mental process that is carried out by our brain is the result of it attempting to increase certainty of self within a given environment, regardless of the actual outcome."

Excited, Rob continued.

"So whether it results in a physical action or not, the desired result of any mental process is to increase the certainty of self relative to one's environment," he repeated it again, hoping that I was beginning to understand.

"Now, I don't know whether it's true or not, but it is a cool theory don't you think? What if everything that we do can be explained by one core statement or theory?" he asked rhetorically, eyes now beaming brightly.

"I'm sorry, I know, I'm an engineer, but the idea that you could describe the human mind in logical terms that are almost mathematical is something that really excites me. And I really feel like it's starting to make sense now. Back in a minute," he said quickly, as he jumped up from the table and headed toward the bar.

I sat there pondering what he was saying. But what he was saying seemed to make a lot more sense to him than I could make of it. How had he reached a point of understanding without me? I still found it difficult to think of my thoughts being considered as actions.

And what was "certainty of self relative to environment"? What did that mean? How could this one statement explain everything we think? As Rob sat back down with a couple more pints of beer, I got straight back into it:

"Okay. Questions: firstly, what or rather how does one 'increase certainty of self relative to environment'?"

He shrugged and answered, "It doesn't matter — that's the point. Once you understand that it is relative to a given environment, then you can understand that it all comes down to how you define or interpret an environment."

He paused for a moment before continuing.

"You could increase certainty through doing anything. Obviously, through eating, drinking, sleeping, and all the usual stuff that we do. But, it could be through any sport or hobby that you increase your certainty. Provided you *believe* you're increasing your certainty and the results of your actions complement that belief, then your mind accepts that it is increasing its certainty. Basically, he is saying that everything the mind does is in some way ultimately to increase certainty. Everything!"

"What about when we make mistakes?" I asked.

"It's only a mistake because we learn that it didn't increase our certainty through our action. But we were attempting to increase our certainty when choosing the action. Right?" he asked, gesticulating with his hands in front of him.

"Okay," I said again, trying to think of something we do that doesn't increase our certainty, "What about drinking excessively? What about drug addiction?" I asked, sure that these deliberate acts don't increase the certainty of our minds relative to environment and almost hopeful that these examples would highlight the error in Rob's assertions.

"I know, it sounds weird," Rob answered. "But I think they can be explained within the statement as well. For example," he said as he sipped on his beer, "doesn't alcohol take away our sense of uncertainty and give us confidence? Doesn't it give us relief from stress?"

He looked at me, waiting for me to respond. When I didn't, he continued.

"Sure, we may act like a fool after too many beers, but from the mind's perspective, a foggy one at that, we have increased the certainty of the mind while under the influence of alcohol. I would say it would be a similar scenario for other drugs. You can't look at a drug addict from your perspective and understand what is going on their mind. You have to ask are they feeling, like they have increased their certainty from their perspective? And from the mind's perspective, it's all about what is happening inside the mind rather than what is happening outside."

"You believe a drug addict thinks that they have increased their certainty while under the influence of it?" I asked doubtfully.

"More than that, I would say the drug rewards the user for an increase in certainty that isn't real. The high they experience is the reward for a change in certainty that never occurred other than in their own mind. That's why some drugs are so dangerous," he said, pausing to take a sip of his beer.

"The important thing to remember is that it is the mind that defines what it believes increases its certainty, and through varying its definition of environment it can, and does, change what it is that it believes will increase certainty as well as what it is that defines its environment."

Hoping I understood, he continued talking, taking another approach.

"Think of a board game, for example," he said. "It doesn't matter what game, really. But in any game, you have a set of rules that define how a player can win as well as how a player loses. Once a player decides to play and decides that they care about winning, then the environment is defined. And if the player wins, they will experience an increase in certainty; but if they lose, they will experience a decrease in certainty."

I must have looked interested, so he continued. "So their actions, within the context of the game, will be to try and win and thus increase their certainty," he concluded with confidence, patiently waiting for me to ask my next question.

I wasn't sure if I agreed with him.

"Look, I don't know if this is how he intended his message to be interpreted. It seems to me that you're changing or redefining how we should use 'certainty' and 'action.' Do you really think that is what he meant?" I asked, still uncomfortable with such new ideas.

"Well, I guess you're right, in a sense," Rob admitted. "These words have definitions already which we could look up to be thorough. But many words are used or interpreted differently depending on the context of use."

Again, he turned to an example.

"Newton's Third Law states that: 'For every action there is an equal and opposite reaction.' He's using the term 'action' within the context of physics and we understand and accept that it has different meaning than in another context. There is nothing unusual about that."

Still determined to help me understand, Rob continued. "I think language has been proven to be something that is dynamic and has been evolving with every generation. The spelling of words changes just as the meaning of words change. Language evolves, and I am quite confident that this is how he was using these words when he spoke with you. It's the only way it makes any sense," he concluded, inhaling a deep breath and looking to me to see if his insight and enthusiasm were getting through to me.

"Alright, what about our emotions then? How does his statement explain our emotions?" I asked.

I really wanted to understand, but I wasn't convinced as yet. It was all a little abstract and it felt like he was trying to explain the mind in terms of a mechanical system like a car rather than the complicated organic lump of grey matter that the brain was. I think my failure to understand made me want to change the subject as well; maybe to avoid admitting that I couldn't grasp the concept.

"Right. I'm glad you asked," Rob said, shuffling through his papers, "because this is where it gets really interesting."

I was impressed with Rob's passion and interest in the subject, I had to admit. He continued, clearly excited about what he was saying.

"The first statement or theory explains why we, or our mind, behaves the way it does. The first statement says that the mind tries to increase certainty of self-relative to environment. I think it's pretty straight forward once you interpret it correctly. But, what happens when the mind makes a mistake, as you mentioned before? What happens when our actions decrease our certainty? What about when we do something that benefits us? How do we know whether something increases our certainty or not? There must be some means of feedback. Something that promotes good decisions and something that helps prevent repetition of bad decisions. So, let me write down the second statement," he said, as he wrote the second statement on a fresh page.

All emotions are created by a change in certainty.

"Okay," he continued after clearing his throat, "So, we experience emotions when good things happen or when bad things happen. What I think — and again, this is just my opinion — is that he is suggesting that our emotions are the result of a change in certainty of self relative to the environment."

"So, if good things happen to us, such as having a party or winning a board game, we feel good because there has been an increase in our certainty. Conversely, when bad things happen, like a car accident or a family tragedy, we are sad because there is a loss in certainty. Remember, there has been a loss of certainty of self within the given environment."

"Okay, so that makes sense for happiness or sadness. You've named two emotions. But, what about all the other emotions that are too countless to list? You can't explain them all with that statement," I said as I tapped on the page.

"No," he said, "but you can use this statement to build a framework for the entire range of emotions that we experience, which is what I started doing last night once I decided I was on the right track."

He sifted through his notepad and pulled some pages out that appeared to have some graphs on them and placed the first one in front of me.

"Okay," he said, fidgeting a little in his chair. "I really hope this makes sense to you. Don't look at the first page yet. But, what I decided last night was that if we're going to talk about a change in certainty, then we have to compare certainty over time. Right?"

I waited for him to continue, which he did.

"Any change that the human mind experiences happens relative to time. It doesn't matter whether we're talking about the change in weather or the change in the level of gas in our fuel tank. We experience change as a function of time. So I decided to try and draw a diagram showing the change in certainty of self relative to time. So this is what I started with," he said as he pointed to the first page.

On the page, there was a simple diagram showing a graph with *Certainty* on one axis and *Time* on the other axis:

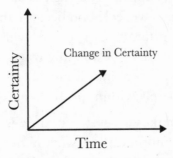

I looked at the diagram and then back at Rob.

"I'm sorry, Rob," I answered, a little disappointed. "Isn't that a tad oversimplified?" I asked, trying not to sound rude. "We're talking about how the mind works and you're drawing a graph showing an arrow."

"I know, I know, I'm an engineer, I do everything in charts and diagrams," he said, chuckling. "It doesn't mean much yet, but this is where I started last night. I asked myself, 'how can I represent the relationship between certainty and time on a piece of paper?' and this is what I drew. But then I asked myself how I could include various emotions such as happiness, sadness, excitement, or anger? What are the real differences between various emotions? And that's when I got really excited."

Again, he sat forward in his chair, eager to help me understand.

"The question that intrigued me was, 'Can our emotions be qualified as well as quantified?' And so I started building on this diagram. It may look a little like a science or math class, but it has really helped me make sense of it. Just be patient and give me a chance to explain."

He paused, sipping on his beer and looking at me enthusiastically.

"You know that you're buying lunch when I finish if it starts making sense to you!" he said, smiling with confidence.

"Okay," he said, continuing, "So, I asked myself what are the aspects of emotions that distinguish one from the other. Happiness and sadness are obviously different because one reflects a positive change in certainty and the other reflects a negative change in certainty. In one case, good things happen and in the other case, bad things happen. When you are happy it is because there has been a positive change in certainty relative to time. Alternatively, when you are sad it is because there has been a negative change in certainty over time. So I drew my graph again. This time I added to the certainty axis that included positive emotions a negative axis to include negative emotions."

He then turned the page and showed me his next drawing:

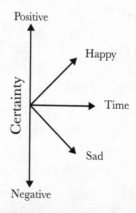

This made a little more sense to me. But I didn't feel that we were moving in the right direction. I could see how if something negative happened, like losing your phone or losing a friend, you might be sad. And, conversely, if you experienced something positive, like having a birthday party or winning the lottery, then you might be happy. It was a nice diagram, sure, but it only covered two emotions and it didn't fill me with much hope for understanding at this stage.

"So, where does excitement fit on your drawing?" I asked doubtfully.

"It doesn't," he said smiling away.

"What do you mean? Aren't you trying to show me how his second statement can be used to explain all emotions?" I asked, somewhat impatiently.

"Yes. So when I looked at this drawing last night, I asked the same thing. I said to myself, 'What's the difference between excitement and happiness?' and that's when the next piece of the puzzle clicked into place. Excitement is something that happens due to the expectation of a change in certainty, as in before it happens, whereas happiness is the result of a change in certainty, occurring *after* the event. Does that make sense?" he asked as he moved to the next piece of paper.

"Look," he said, trying to get my attention as he was pointing at the paper. "I've added time before the change in certainty or event occurs. I've put excitement before the event and happiness after the event. Think about it. We are excited about something good that will happen and we are happy when it does happen. Meaning you can divide emotions into ones that happen before an event, as in predictive, or ones that happen as a result of a change, as in resultant."

I looked at the new page in front of me, considering what he'd said.

I looked at the drawing.

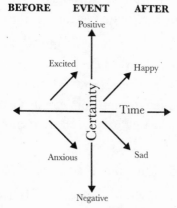

"But if all emotions are created by a change in certainty. How can there be emotions before the event occurs?" I asked, feeling like there was a fairly big hole in his theory.

"It's because your mind has already calculated the likelihood of the event occurring using its imagination and has predicted what is about to happen," Rob explained patiently.

"Once it accepts that something is probably going to happen, it experiences a change in certainty. Our mind choses to test out various scenarios using its imagination combined with its memory to predict what effect a future event will have on its level of certainty. Thus helping it take the correct action depending on what is about to happen. Do you see what I'm getting at?" he asked, without waiting for a response.

"Through predicting a future event a change in certainty occurs within the mind to warn against or promote interest even before any event occurs. Like the mind experiences a change in certainty even when simulating a future event. Of course, it isn't certain of what will happen, so the emotions are predictive only. But, when it concludes that something is going to happen then it may also experience resultant emotions," he finished, pausing for a moment.

"Okay," he continued "how would we know to jump out of the way of a car if we didn't get scared before it hit us? Our mind measures the chance of the car hitting us and warns us through excitement or fear. Fear is what warns us that something will negatively change our certainty if we are not careful."

So far, so good. This part made sense. Rob continued.

"I think you can divide emotions between predictive emotions (those that occur before an event based on likelihood of event) and resultant emotions (those that occur as a result of a definite change in certainty). Sure, you can be sad before an event occurs, but that is only once you determine it is inevitable. Therefore, you're sad because the change in certainty has, for all intensive purpose, already occurred within the mind."

He sat back now and I tried to digest these new ideas. While it all seemed a little overly simplified, it was beginning to feel logical. If you look at certainty as a state of mind and look at change as something that influences our state of certainty, it all came across as quite valid.

"And you think you can fit all emotions into this structure that you've drawn?" I asked, more curiously than earlier as his ideas started to take hold.

"I think so. I've only just started, but I think you can see already that his words make sense in these limited examples. Even if this is just a simple technique for understanding emotions, it's a great way to rationalize what is going on in our minds. Don't you think?" he asked, getting more involved in the ideas as he went.

"Maybe," I said, acknowledging a degree of doubt. It all seemed a little overwhelming. I was caught off-guard by these new concepts. They sounded simple enough. I just struggled to decide whether they made sense for me.

"What do you mean?" he said, "Look at how these words, these concepts, have helped you resolve your mental conflicts!" Rob said, eager to make his point.

"You yourself have already applied his ideas — you just don't understand how. What if his theories really do explain how our minds work? Man, I want to meet this guy and shake his hand. Surely as an end user of the human mind, it is in our best interest to understand how it works. What if, through understanding how it works, we are able to live a happier and more fulfilled life? Don't you see it?"

And here, Rob showed genuine excitement. "Whether we're talking about a philosophy or getting closer to real understanding of the human mind, these principles are like the beginnings of an instruction manual for the human mind," he continued with confidence.

"I guess I like what you're saying, but for every answer you give, I have another twenty questions. For example, happiness is a generalization for a whole range of degrees of happiness, as is sadness, for that matter. How can you explain that on your diagram?" I asked, still not convinced.

"That's easy," he said, drawing some more lines on the last page we were looking at. "The strength of an emotion or in other words the degree of happiness you feel will be based upon how much change occurs relative to time. Meaning that as the rate of change in certainty increases so does the strength of the emotion. Look here," he said, pointing at the page again.

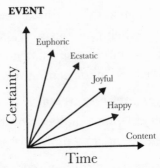

"Now," he said, pointing at the different levels of happiness. "I've only put in some ideas for positive emotions. But you can see that you can do the same thing for negative emotions. And it doesn't matter exactly how you draw it. What I'm trying to show is that as the rate of change in certainty increases so does the strength of the emotion. What next?" he finished, throwing his pen on the table and leaning back in his chair. "I'm on a roll."

"Okay," I said, trying to catch him out now as his confidence was building. The way I saw it we'd barely touched the surface. "What about anger? I don't see how that fits in to your system. Where does that fit into your drawing?"

"Bugger," he said, looking a little disappointed. "You got me there. I was thinking about it late last night but I hadn't worked that one out yet."

He wrote down "Anger" on the pad and looked back at me.

"That, my friend, will have to wait for another day. My brain is already fried from all this self-analysis. It's exhausting thinking about thought! What do you say we grab some lunch? Whose shout is it anyway?" he asked, trying to determine whether I was satisfied with his overnight thesis that I'd assigned to him.

"Well, I think you've earned yourself lunch on me. I must say I wasn't expecting all of this," I said, pointing to the notepad.

"No offense," I continued. "But I definitely didn't think you'd come back with mathematical diagrams showing types of emotions. This is great! I think I agree with everything you've said. I just need time to digest it. Can I keep the pages and review them later?" I asked.

"Sure, I've got them up here," Rob said confidently, pointing at his head.

"You know, I've solved a lot of engineering puzzles, but this stuff is really interesting. I never would have thought that you could explain the mind using simple statements or diagrams." He seemed genuinely excited about what he had uncovered.

"I don't know whether it's just me trying to fit my understanding of the human mind within the context of engineering principles or whether it is actually that the mind, like any system, that can be explained in engineering terms."

He continued, saying, "I mean, I know what I've shown you is very simple. The point is that I think that I believe and understand your friend on the hill," pausing for dramatic emphasis.

"The fact that I cannot explain anger within my theory is not because it's not possible; I just need more time. I have to tell you, I'm quite excited about this 'mind' project you've got me involved in. Cheers!" he said jovially, and we toasted to the success of our "adventures" so far.

Yes, it was an adventure. We were venturing into the unknown. No maps or books to tell us where we were, or what to expect. Isn't that what an adventure is? Sure, most adventures involve exploring our environment, but understanding our own minds is one of the last remaining unexplored frontiers.

Surely, understanding self should be one of the first things we learn. I pondered the significance of these new concepts while we ordered lunch. Why didn't we understand how the mind works when we understood the environment we lived in so well? Understanding self must allow us to adapt to our environment more effectively. What if a deeper degree of understanding of how the mind works allows us to deal with our emotions more effectively?

Rob pulled me out of my reverie as the waitress took our orders. We changed the line of conversation while we ate lunch and it was interesting to hear about the barman's different perspective on life.

He seemed to see the world through different eyes than most people. His life philosophy was like that of a Buddhist engineer — if there is such a thing — who is trying to make the world a happier place, one person at a time, through the use of positive logic.

It seemed like every problem he came across provided an opportunity to study the most positive approach and solution. We talked about our travels and our professions and by the end of lunch, I felt like I'd really connected with Rob.

After lunch we parted ways, but not before we agreed to further discussion over lunch the following day — only this time he agreed to buy lunch. I decided to go for an afternoon walk and explore some of the streets around the Edinburgh Castle. After absorbing so much important, new information, a change of scenery would do me good.

I peered into shop windows and occasionally ventured into them to look at something that caught my eye, but mostly I was just wandering around the tourist area, letting my mind unwind.

So, after a heavy pub lunch and a couple of beers, I felt relaxed enough to begin to reflect on how Rob had divided emotions based on qualities: Positive & negative, predictive & resultant, and varying strength based on the rate of change in certainty.

On the one hand, it sounded logical but on the other, I still couldn't fully capture what "change in certainty" was. It lingered in my thoughts, surfacing again and again: *What is "change in certainty"?*

This much I knew for sure: If you could define emotions based on specific qualities, then every emotion must be definable using this system. If I could test the system for each emotion, then it would either prove valid or invalid.

Using this method, I could prove whether Rob was right or wrong, couldn't I? And, in doing so, perhaps validate my friend the Magician's statements at the same time. The questions kept surfacing in my mind now, arriving rapidly.

Were Rob's ideas evidence that the Magician was right? It *felt* like he was right. But at what point would I be satisfied with either of their explanations?

As I walked through various streets in Edinburgh Old Town, I was content to let my mind wander as well as my legs. I was happy with life, and relaxed — and I had no place to be until that evening.

How can we analyze emotions, anyway? It seemed like a "Catch 22" scenario. How can we understand an emotion without experiencing it first? And even when we experience the emotion, we are so involved in how it makes us feel that it is virtually impossible to examine the analytical, mechanical aspects of it.

When we experience dark, uncomfortable emotions, the last thing we want to do is dwell in those emotions or try to better understand them. And when we are happy, excited, or ecstatic, we just want to enjoy ourselves.

How, then, do we experience and process our emotions in a way that allows us to see if it fits into any kind of system? Surely, the fact that we are experiencing an emotion inhibits our ability to rationalize it. Maybe that explains why most of us don't understand our emotions better.

As I stepped out onto the road at a small intersection, I was suddenly confronted by a cyclist who braked suddenly and began yelling at me. I stepped back quickly and, looking around, realized that I'd stepped out onto the road without looking at the traffic lights.

I was totally in the wrong and suddenly realized how close we both were to experiencing a painful, perhaps tragic, accident. It shook me, as you can imagine, and as the courier rode off swearing curses (that I couldn't make out because of his thick accent) I also felt a sense of embarrassment.

So I got myself off the road and decided to stop somewhere for a quick coffee, to calm my nerves. I found a nice little café on the same street and as I sat there gazing out the window, warming up, I thought about my near-miss on the road.

I was very lucky it was only a cyclist and not a car. Where had my head been? Well, I knew it had been drifting between thoughts. How many beers had I drunk at lunch? Clearly, I was distracted at the time. But the experience had given me quite a scare. I could still feel my heart racing.

Alright, so if I'd just experienced the emotion of feeling frightened, could I now place this emotion on Rob's diagram, as he suggested? I unfolded the sheets from my pocket and found the right page.

I'd "gotten a scare" or "gotten a fright" before getting hit and that had made me jump back from the street. It had been sudden, yes, but the sudden act had helped me avoid being hit by the bike. It made sense that fear, in this case, was a negative predictive emotion designed to prevent something bad from happening. It made simple sense!

As I worked this through in my head, I suddenly started to understand and believe what Rob was saying. It started to dawn on me that the emotion I'd just experienced — fear — was there to protect me from the oncoming accident; my mind's way of saying, "Hey James, move out of the way! Something bad is about to happen!"

I felt uplifted, seeing my experience in this knew light. Who was it giving me this warning, though? Was it my subconscious mind?

Then I started thinking about the cyclist and how angry he'd been. He looked like a local courier in a rush to get from one office to another to drop off documents or some such. I'd stepped out onto the road and nearly ruined his day. I could see why he was angry. He was angry at me because I was in the wrong. My actions had nearly turned his day from a normal work day to one that included potential harm; either to his bike, to his body, or to both.

As I studied the diagram more closely, I saw Rob's writing in capitals: ANGER. He'd left his reminder on the pages he'd given me. I think I would be angry too, but as I studied the page, I was unclear about anger as an emotion and why it was different than the other emotions in the diagram.

Suddenly, a light bulb turned on in my mind. "That's it!" I said to myself, with a rush of excitement. Now I had a reason for Rob to buy lunch tomorrow. The difference was clear: Rob's diagram only showed what happened when there was an event that was about to occur. It didn't show what would happen if someone's *action* was about to produce a change in certainty.

If an event occurred in the courier's environment that could not be associated to someone's actions, who would he be angry at? Anger seemed to be an emotion he experienced when someone's actions reduced his certainty.

So anger was the result of a negative change in certainty as a result of actions, rather than an event. Maybe that even included our own actions. In this case, my action's almost produced a loss in certainty. The courier couldn't be angry at bad weather. He could only be angry at the choices that led to him experiencing the bad weather. So, you can't be angry at an event, but you can be angry at someone's choice of action.

Yet, I still could not see how to fit anger onto the current diagram without adding "action" as the cause of the change in certainty. It seemed that a change in certainty could be produced in three different circumstances. An incident had to occur that produced a change in certainty through:

1. An event (every day occurrences not associated to our actions)

2. Someone's actions (self or someone else)

3. A combination of both event and action (typical situations)

I then crossed out "Event" on one of his diagrams and wrote "Action." I also changed "sad" to "angry." I looked at the diagram in satisfaction

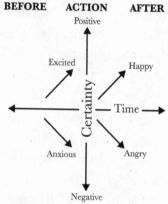

Anger, it seemed, was a reaction to someone's actions that have had a negative impact on another person. Like it was there to promote a response to regain the certainty that had been taken by someone or something that we could target as the cause of change. So, I made a note of this idea below the diagram:

Anger is a negative reactive resultant emotion.

That's not to say that I might not be sad due to someone's actions. Only in the case of the event, there was nothing I could do to change the negative outcome.

I also noted that an event seemed to be anything outside of our control — and an action was anything within our control.

For example, we might be sad if a party was cancelled due to weather. But if we missed a party due to someone's actions such as being given the wrong time or address then it is more likely that we would be angry.

Now I was really beginning to feel like his diagrams made sense. I wondered what other emotions were dependent on action rather than event. I wondered whether this would make sense the following day, after my big night out "Edinburgh" style.

As I looked at the diagram, I wondered whether happiness should be changed to gratitude or thankfulness. But as I often happens while focusing on elements of the human mind, my own mind started to drift — almost as if full understanding was deliberately trying to elude me just when I thought I'd found it.

We celebrated that night with the local Edinburgh crowd. As I sat chatting with friends, I let the world take me for a ride wherever it wanted to. I watched locals fight and laughed at jokes that I couldn't understand. The more I laughed, the more I enjoyed the liberty of living without worry and depression. It felt good to be free … finally.

I can't tell you how things ended up that night. I laugh every time I think about singing the Scottish national anthem with my best friend and a local policeman as we ate burgers at a fast-food stand. What I can tell you is that we had a tremendous night out on the town, and somehow I made it back to my hotel — possibly with some help from the policeman we'd met at the burger stand.

Chapter VI

Misdirection

*A*t the intermission, the Engineer, along with many patrons, filed into the main foyer where champagne and hors d'oeuvres were being served. There was a string quartet playing classical music at the base of the main staircase. It was an inviting break from tonight's show.

As he made his way to the end of the bar, carefully weaving his way between various-sized parties, he heard many people sharing comments and queries on the evening's performance. After he'd ordered a glass of champagne he stepped to one side, where he could gaze across the great theatre foyer without intrusion.

This was one of his favorite parts of the evening. It was strange, but he enjoyed being around the people and enjoying their excitement almost as much as the pleasure he himself derived from the performance. Their happiness and energy touched him; it gave the performance meaning and significance. Even when some of the audience had cried out in fear or surprise during the first act, he'd felt their emotion almost as if it were his.

It was like he'd learned more about the patrons just by watching and listening than if he were to engage in conversation with them. He felt as if understanding the audience gave insight into the Magician's performance. It seemed to affirm his own feelings about the performance; in fact, they echoed his own belief.

As he stood sipping on a glass of champagne, soaking in the ambience of his surroundings, he couldn't ignore the particular glow of energy and excitement that the patrons were giving off this evening. Every week, there were different performances, ranging from operas to theatricals to orchestral performances. It wasn't uncommon for there to be a magic show, either, but for some reason tonight felt different. It was something that the Engineer was sure he could sense, although he didn't know the meaning of it.

His eyes wandered from group to group as he inspected their dresses, suits and various accoutrements. He watched their faces, studied their eyes as they lit up with enthusiasm; their cheeks flush with emotion. Out on the streets, people's faces were bland, cold, empty of expression or feeling. But in this special place, you could see that they were alive. This is why people came to the theatre, it was certainly why he came.

He didn't come to the theatre as often as he desired. If there was a project that he was contracted to complete then he would not allow such distractions to enter his mind. But in between contracts, he would sometimes come as often as every other night; sometimes every night — even if he'd seen the show previously.

Suddenly and without notice, someone bumped into him from behind. His thoughts were quickly brought back to the moment. He turned to exchange apologies with his fellow patron and after excusing himself he was confronted by a lovely young woman who, funnily enough, looked very similar to the Magician's assistant, yet was dressed like one of the patrons.

"I'm sorry," she said, politely, "But I think you dropped this."

And she smiled with innocent sincerity as she placed the handkerchief in his suit jacket pocket. As he looked down it was immediately apparent that there had been a mistake. But before he could tell her that it didn't belong to him, she was disappearing into the crowd; something she seemed to do incredibly well as he lost sight of her in the crowd almost immediately.

As he looked down and inspected the handkerchief once more, he was confronted by a large E on its corner. It looked so familiar that he had to wonder whether it was his after all. Yet handkerchiefs were not something he chose to use either for function or fashion. Having said that, he quite liked the look of the handkerchief in his pocket; his personal logo as part of his attire. As a sign of acceptance, he straightened the strange gift in his pocket so that the embroidery read clearly.

The first of two reminders sounded for the patrons to return to their seats. The quartet was no longer playing by the staircase and as he finished his champagne and made his way back to his seat, he thought to himself: tonight was particular indeed.

Chapter 7

The Silent Companion

*T*he following day started with the realization that my body and mind were suffering. It was an instantaneous awareness that the rest of the day wasn't going to be my best. My displeasure with the day increased in dissatisfying increments.

First of all, I noticed dryness in my mouth with the unpleasant taste of alcohol and hamburger still lingering. Then, as I stumbled to the bathroom and looked in the mirror trying to see why my head ached so much, I noticed that my eyes didn't want to accept that I was awake. And when I finally looked at myself in the mirror, the view only emphasized my sorry state.

I tried to go back to bed but made the mistake of looking at my watch on the way there. It was 11:30 a.m. — and I was scheduled to be meeting Rob at noon. What had I been thinking? Why hadn't I arranged to meet at 2 p.m. or even 5 p.m.? I really didn't feel like leaving the hotel, but I knew I'd regret it if I didn't meet up with him.

After struggling with this decision, I eventually built up the courage to face the day and got myself ready. With minimal attention to detail I showered, dressed and grabbed my notes as I walked out the door. At least I didn't have too far to go.

I made it to the pub right at midday and ordered a strong coffee. Rob had not yet arrived, but I was quite happy to sit and vegetate while trying to revive myself with the help of caffeine.

You know those days when you're aware that you aren't fit to be out among others and yet you somehow find yourself sitting among the normal folk? This was one of those days. I promised myself never to repeat this error, knowing full well this would not be the last time. Still, I really felt that I had to meet with Rob one last time before heading back to London. Why did hangovers have to be so horrible? I mean, I know your body is trying to recover from last night's punishment.

I know the alcohol basically poisons your body. But, did it have to be that bad? Even adding sugar to my coffee seemed to be a long, drawn-out process that required far too much effort and concentration. I tried to focus as I told my hands to pour the packet of sugar into my cup. My hand shook slightly, spilling some of the sugar onto the table. I started to get irritated by my brain's lack of cooperation. The connection between mind and body was fragile at best. All I could do was try to pretend everything was normal.

It was like half my brain was still asleep and the other half didn't have enough brain power to maintain control. I was reminded of my location when I heard a chair sliding on the floor as Rob sat down to join me. He'd appeared out of nowhere. The speed of his movement was displeasing, as it only emphasized that he (rather than I) was in a proper mental state.

"Wow, you look great!" he said, with an ironic chuckle. "You must have had a big night. Surprised you made it at all!"

"I didn't want to," I admitted. "How are you doing?" I asked as I sipped on my coffee.

"Good. I have some more ideas that I think are pretty cool," he answered.

"Me, too!" I tried to respond enthusiastically. "I think I worked something out yesterday after I left you. I will have to remind myself what it was though, as my head is a little cloudy today." I sifted through my pad trying to find the right page. One of the pages fell to the floor and I feebly bent down to pick it up.

"Are you sure you're up to this?" Rob asked as I sat back upright and rubbed my aching head.

"Yeah, I'll be fine. Maybe we could do a change of venue though? I wouldn't mind one last hike up to Arthur's Seat. I think the fresh air might help," I suggested.

"Great. If we're lucky, we may even bump into your friend," Rob offered as we got up to go.

"I'd like that. It would be great for you guys to meet each other," I said.

"Also be nice to say 'cheerio,'" I added.

"When do you head back to London?" he asked, as we made our way through the streets with the hilltop in sight above the rows of terrace houses.

"I have an early train tomorrow morning. I think sometime around 7 a.m. So it will be an early night for me!" I said with a dry chuckle.

"Well, make sure you keep in touch, eh," he said genuinely.

"Yeah, I will. Maybe we can share our discoveries by e-mail?" I suggested.

"Sounds like a plan," he said.

We both knew that today wasn't going to be our last discussion. We knew that we would be able to continue our study of the human mind together. It also took away some of the finality of today's meeting and removed some of the urgency to share our ideas. I was still excited about introducing my latest ideas to Rob and I was sure that he felt the same.

But without making any agreement, we both held off talking about our discoveries until we reached the hilltop. Maybe it was partly so we could focus on the task at hand uninterrupted. And maybe there was a part of both of us that was hoping the Magician would be there and we could share our ideas with him.

When we reached the top, though, there was no sign of him. There was a variety other folk, including hikers, some joggers and an occasional mountain biker — but there was no Magician. We both brushed aside our disappointment and accepted that we would not be honored with his cryptic insights.

We found ourselves a spot to sit, away from the track but not quite on the cliff edge where I'd sat two days earlier. There was a slight breeze so it wasn't ideal for going through our notepads, but we were too enthusiastic about sharing our scribblings to become frustrated by the weather.

As we settled ourselves on the hilltop for the last time, I could still picture the Magician repeating his rules for understanding the human mind:

"All actions are taken to increase certainty."

&

"All emotions are created by a change in certainty."

He may not have been there on the hill chuckling away but I felt that he would always be present in my thoughts, as it was his ideas that had inserted themselves into my conscious mind and affected me so profoundly.

"So, who's going to start?" asked Rob, bringing me back to reality.

"I think it has to be my turn to start today," I said. "How about I go first?"

"Fire away!" Rob added enthusiastically.

"Well, yesterday, after I left you, I went for a stroll around town. I wanted to clear my head and I found myself thinking about what you'd said at lunch. I guess I must have been deep in my own thoughts because I forgot to look before stepping into a busy intersection. I nearly got run over by one of the couriers that ride the mountain bikes around town. Do you know the ones I mean?" I asked.

"Yeah, I know the ones," Rob answered. "They're the quickest guys in town. Great way to move documents if you're in a rush. You're lucky you didn't get hurt! — before or after the incident. They can be very aggressive if they're trying to get somewhere fast," he said earnestly.

"Right. Anyway, he was pretty angry with me and when

I sat down to take a break and get out of the cold, I started thinking about what anger was and what was different about the emotion compared to the ones we discussed earlier," I told him.

"And it just came to me as I was analyzing the situation that had just occurred. I could see what was different," I said, pausing briefly before beginning again.

"The emotion of anger requires a loss in certainty due to someone or something's actions. Nobody gets angry at the weather when they get stuck in the rain, for example. They get angry at themselves or someone else for getting them into this situation."

I could feel the pieces of the puzzle coming together, even as I spoke.

"It's only when our actions or the actions of others affect us that we experience anger," I continued.

"The cyclist was angry at me because my daydreaming nearly ruined his day. Meaning, anger is always directed at someone or something, even when you're angry at yourself. So, I decided that anger is not only a negative resultant emotion but also a reactive emotion, rather than being passive like sadness. In the case of an event, you can't change what has happened. There is no one to blame; it's out of your control. In the case of someone's actions reducing your certainty, you get angry because your mind wants to get back the certainty that has been taken. Your change in certainty is within your control."

Rob listened carefully, then responded.

"I like it," he said. "I must admit, I've seen people get angry with objects but it doesn't really make sense. You can't blame an inanimate object or a force of nature for your problems."

He reflected for a moment before continuing.

"I've seen a man kick a train on the London underground after the train sat in the tunnel for fifteen minutes with all of us crammed in like sardines, no air to breathe. I don't think he was angry with the train, though; he just needed to kick something to relieve his anger towards someone he could not see or blame for his claustrophobic experience."

I listened to Rob carefully, and he continued.

"But that still doesn't explain where anger sits in the current spectrum of emotions we have drawn up. Where does it fit in the framework that we have so far?"

"Well," I responded, "I think it occurs after an incident. In the case of the cyclist, he was angry after the near-miss because at some point, he believed it would happen and therefore experienced the loss of certainty, I guess. It's obviously negative. He was certainly not happy with me. But instead of him being sad because an event occurred that wasn't based on someone's actions, he experienced anger because it was my actions that nearly caused the accident. So, we are passive when there is no one at fault. I mean, what choice do we have? But we are more reactive when there is someone that has taken certainty from us. Does that sound right?" I asked, unsure of myself.

"I love it," Rob responded with genuine enthusiasm. "Passive emotions due to events where no one is at fault and reactive emotions when someone's actions take away our certainty. This falls in with what I was working on last night. So, for a change in certainty to occur it could be due to someone's actions (including your own) or through an event occurring or through a combination of both — which is more likely in most cases," said Rob, echoing my thoughts from yesterday.

"Right, that's what I was thinking. It's all about how we perceive the change in certainty. Is it through our actions, someone else's actions, or through an event that cannot be assigned to anyone?"

I took a breath, then continued. "Just because someone caused a negative change in certainty doesn't mean you'll get angry. Some people get angry; others might get sad. It's all a question of whether you accept that a change is permanent or whether your instinct is to fight against the change. As in, do we use fight or flight when we are confronted with a negative change in certainty? In the first situation, there is the belief that our actions can regain certainty, meaning it is within our ability to control. In the second, there is the belief that the loss in certainty is permanent, meaning that the change is out of our control."

I paused for a moment to look at Rob as we both tried to download these new ideas. It seemed odd that anger was the only reactive emotion I could think of.

"What is the positive alternative to anger?" I asked, deferring my question to Rob.

"Appreciation? Gratitude? I don't know. What about love? Is that not a positive reactive emotion that we experience when someone increases our certainty?" he offered, not looking sure of himself.

"I don't know. Maybe. But we get angry more readily and with more people than we fall in love with."

And then, I made a prediction: "I think when I get back

to London, I'm going to look up every emotion and try to test each emotion based on our ideas so far," realizing that we were getting into areas where we had not investigated yet. "Any other discoveries over night?" I asked, hoping for more from the engineer and the man who had become my friend.

"Well, I've got some ideas that I'm working on but I'm not confident yet, so I think I'll hold onto them for now," he said, with a smile.

"There's something else I still can't get my head around," I stated, "Why does he say that *all* actions are taken to increase certainty? Why not just *some* actions?"

I'd given it quite a bit of thought and really wanted to discuss this angle with Rob. I continued, saying, "I think I agree that any time we experience a change in certainty, there will be an emotional response proportional to how we perceive that change in certainty. I still have a lot of thinking to do on the second statement, but I feel comfortable with it. The first statement, however, just seems too absolute. How can every action that we choose be taken to increase certainty? That's what I can't seem to get my head around." I looked at the engineer to see if he'd gained greater insight on this than me.

"I know what you're saying," he said. "But it's easier to understand if you focus on how you define 'action' relative to the mind. The mind experiences change in certainty whether it originates from a change in the environment or from a change within the mind. The source might be different but the *effect* can be the same."

A gentle breeze blew across our papers, shuffling them lightly, but Rob continued. "I mean, the mind can only perceive change in certainty as something that occurs within the mind. Everything that the mind experiences is a projection of the mind. In the same way 'action' is really defined by that step that the mind takes in order to increase certainty."

He paused for a moment before continuing. "You could say that an action is any process, mental or physical, that is carried out by the mind to increase certainty. Alternately, you could say that all mental processes are taken to increase certainty."

He waited momentarily to see if his words were sinking in. I guess the expression on my face confirmed that he needed to continue with his explanation.

"Alright. We think of actions as physical processes that we carry out such as walking, running, speaking, swimming, etc. However, from the perspective of the mind, all processes occur within the mind. The mind distinguishes mental processes and physical processes, but it experiences all processes within itself. So it interprets the results of these processes within the mind as well."

"So from the mind's perspective," he continued, "an action is just defined as the process that it chooses to increase certainty, meaning certainty of self within a given environment. The mind attempts to increase certainty through action. Change in certainty produces emotion that is proportionate to the change. The mind choses different actions to increase certainty given the current emotion like a feedback loop. The greater the strength of the emotion, the more it will impact on the choice of the mind's actions. Does that make more sense?" he asked in his usual sincere and patient manner.

"The way you explain it makes sense. I'm not sure if it will still make sense tomorrow, but I think I have it. I just have to alter how I think of 'action' rather than trying to fit my preconception of it into his model of how the mind works." I looked around at that point, hoping to see him.

"Do you believe he meant that this is really how the mind works or is he just suggesting a philosophy?" I asked Rob.

"I don't know," he answered honestly. "Does it matter? Whether you treat it as a simplified guide to the mind or if you take it as the basis of all thought, it creates a framework for understanding self."

"It allows us to explore the concept of 'certainty' and how our certainty is affected by change," he continued. "What do we possess that defines our level of certainty within our environment? What changes will affect our level of certainty? What do we believe will make us happy compared to what will *actually* make us happy?"

"I'm not concerned whether it is a philosophy or a type of scientific theory. Maybe it's just a logical starting point for any of us to explore our own thoughts and feelings. I mean, we've only been talking about it for a couple of days. I guess, like any theory, it needs to be tested over time to establish its validity," he suggested, correctly, pausing in thought.

"I think it's all relative," I offered, "Understanding how every neuron is connected within the brain doesn't help us understand how to live a happy life. However, understanding how the mind experiences happiness through a positive change in certainty does give us greater opportunity to be happy."

"I think you're right; shame we haven't seen the Magician," he commented, using my name for my friend the sage. "I'd like to meet him one day. You say that he's changed your life.

I think I feel the same. I feel like I understand myself better now that I have a way of analyzing my thoughts, actions and emotions."

We both sat looking out across the landscape.

"Thanks for getting me involved, James," Rob said sincerely. "Thanks for bringing me into your adventure. I've never talked about this side of life with anyone. But I really enjoyed it. I think it might be my new hobby," he said, shaking my hand and giving me a pat on the shoulder.

And that was how I remember ending our conversations about the mind with Rob. We chatted amiably as we walked back into town, but it was just light conversation. Even with my hangover, though, I felt content. My mind was clear once more and I felt ready for anything. I definitely felt ready for London life again. I was ready to start living once more.

As we made our way through the streets of Edinburgh, Rob and I agreed to keep in contact and share our ideas when we could through email. I wished him luck with his studies and said "cheerio" once we had arrived back at the "local" then headed off to meet Simon, who I could only hope was feeling better than me.

The coffee and the walk had helped a lot and I was feeling at least halfway on the road to recovery from last night.

And that's how I wrapped up my holiday in Edinburgh. I spent the rest of the day relaxing and laughing about the previous night with Simon and company. I was content, free, and positive. Can any of us ask for more? All I wanted in my last few hours in Edinburgh was to soak in as much of the local ambience as I could. Oh, Flower of Scotland, when would I see your likes again?

I wrapped things up with the hotel that evening so I could make an early get away in the morning. I packed my bags and looked over the room one last time before collapsing onto the bed one last time. It had been a wonderful trip.

That night, I found my thoughts wandering as I attempted to fall asleep. My thoughts were a mix of memories from my week in Edinburgh: vivid memories of my brief encounters with the Magician; blurred memories of my evenings out, and happy memories of all the little experiences I'd had that inspired me and made Edinburgh so special.

I don't remember falling asleep that evening. Not that I normally would. But as the curtains closed on one performance ... they opened on another.

Chapter *VII*

The Grand Illusion

*D*arkness once more surrounded the Engineer. Without form or feature, it permeated through the space around him. Muffled sounds in the darkness hinted at the surroundings. But the darkness was so absolute that it would be easy to become disoriented.

As the Engineer waited patiently, he could see the stage lights start to glow. As the lights started to illuminate the stage, the gentle sound of a harp could be heard playing some pleasant folk song. The show was starting once more.

As overhead spotlights were directed toward the center of the stage, the Magician returned, welcomed back by the audience as they cheered and clapped in respect. He walked gracefully to the front of the stage while pausing to bow in appreciation every few steps, focusing his attention on different parts of the crowd.

It was clear that he wished to address the audience

as he had at the commencement of the first half of his performance. Once more, he waited patiently for the crowd to settle and for all eyes to focus on him. The harp continued to play softly in the background with a subtle, hypnotic tone. As he looked around the audience he smiled with a look of placid contentment.

"Ladies and gentlemen," he announced, "We are but halfway along tonight's journey. Many of you have experienced the rare delight of magic this evening. You have been thrilled; amazed; some even scared, if but for a moment."

He paused for affect, looking at one of the ladies who had screamed during a previous trick. She blushed, covering her face with her gloved hand.

"You have seen that which is not possible and yet your mind desperately tries to explain that which is inexplicable; you attempt to rationalize that which cannot be rational."

He paused again, allowing the harp's melody to drift through the air.

"I would like to tell you a secret, if I may," he said with a hint of mystery in his voice. "A deep truth about each and every one of you that you choose to deny in case it destroys you."

Pausing again, he gazed at the audience intently before continuing. "Your reality, the place that you live, is a flimsy, two-dimensional fabric. I know I am being rude. But you all believe you can distinguish between that which is real and that which is unreal. Like there is a line between them that you're aware of."

The crowd sat mesmerized, and he continued. "But, as you can see from tonight's show, your reality is easily corrupted by the unreal without you being able to tell the difference."

He paused once more, looking around the audience, looking at each patron with his dark, penetrating eyes.

"In truth, your reality is but a belief. It is not just one belief, it is a multitude of beliefs. Forgive me if I am being too abstract. But clearly, you're too confident in your interpretation of reality. You think you know what you see to be real, and yet I have already shown you the vulnerability of your beliefs. If you're not convinced, I beg you to observe my simple hat," and he took off his hat, presenting it to the crowd, twirling it between his hands.

"It is but a simple hat; it is not special in any way. Please take it," he said to the patrons in the front row. "Inspect it, hold it, look inside it. Madam: if you care to sit on it, I will take no offense. Please," he insisted, "so that the rest of the audience can see that it is but a simple hat."

And as he spoke, the lady in the front row stood up and then, with a childish grin, sat down gingerly on top of the Magician's hat. The audience all chuckled at the spectacle.

"Thank you," said the Magician. "Now, if you will be so kind as to give me my hat." He waited patiently as the gentleman next to the lady reached up with the compressed hat.

"So, as you can see it is but a simple hat. Until!" he exclaimed, "Until you give it to me ... and then it becomes magical," he said, as he punched the hat back into shape, drawing his hand back out of the hat and holding the traditional white rabbit. A few in the audience gave a cheer.

"But, in all honesty, it is not the hat that is magical," he said, as he replaced his hat on his head and gently patted the rabbit. "It is the rabbit. But how can the rabbit be magical if it is really a dove?" he asked as he threw it up into the air.

The rabbit had vanished; in its place, a white dove flew up above the crowd in wide circles. The audience let out a cry of surprise, followed by applause.

"So, am I telling you the truth or do I deceive you? You see that it is not the hat that is magical, or the rabbit, or even the dove. The magic, and this is the secret I've been trying to get to," he said, reminding the audience of his earlier promise. "The magic is in each and every one of you."

He paused for dramatic emphasis.

"Because all that I do is manipulate your assumptions about what is real and what is unreal and present them in conflict. The magic is in finding the weaknesses in your beliefs, finding the conflicts, and presenting them together in opposition," he said softly, gazing into the audience.

"A hat cannot be sat upon with a rabbit inside. A hat cannot be flat with a rabbit inside. If I reach into an empty hat, I cannot pull a rabbit from it. Nor can a rabbit transform into a dove. And yet, you have all witnessed these impossibilities."

He paused again as the dove flew back and landed on his hand, which he swiftly handed to his female assistant.

"You see, the illusion is not here on stage. The illusion is sitting in the audience. Maybe sitting next to you or maybe sitting in front. Because the illusion is in your certainty in belief."

The audience leaned forward, eager to understand, and the Magician continued.

"Each and every one of you are so confident that you know what you see to be true. You think I am playing with you," he chuckled pleasantly.

"But, of course I am. Did you not come to be entertained? But, the fact remains that you're all certain that you know the difference between real and unreal. It is this presumption of certainty that I use to weave my magic. You put too much faith in your senses."

He paused once more to allow the audience to consider his words.

"It is your beliefs that allow me to elicit the rollercoaster of emotions you each experience. It is through challenging your sense of certainty that I can generate disbelief. That is the truth behind my magic."

He paused now, smiling at the audience with a cheeky, if not devious, smile.

"So, for my last trick tonight I would like to play a game with you. I would like you all to stand up if you believe that I am here in front of you."

As he waited, the audience sat and looked around in uncertainty from one to another.

"Please, ladies and gents," he said earnestly. "I would like anyone in the audience that believes I am here on stage in front of you to stand up."

Now the audience started to get up one by one even though, to many, it seemed like a silly joke. The Magician looked around as he waited. He didn't speak to the crowd directly but through various gestures he questioned and encouraged those that had not moved until all but a few in the audience were standing.

"So it would appear that nearly all of you believe that I stand in front of you right now. You're certain that I am in front of you on stage?" he asked, and stomped his foot on the stage to emphasize his point.

"Then what better way for me to show you the truth in magic than for me to demonstrate the falsity of your belief? If the secret to magic is finding the flaws in your beliefs and juxtaposing that which is real with that which is unreal, then what if I could show you that *I am not here at all?*"

And with that, the Magician spun on his feet, wrapping his cloak around himself as he did. He spun faster and faster, concealed by the cloak. Gradually getting closer and closer to the stage until all that was left was the hat and cloak sitting on the flat stage. He'd vanished.

The audience looked around in surprise and confusion. From up in the second tier, the Magician's voice called out across the audience: "And that, my dear friends, is why it is called magic!"

As the audience all turned, they could see that the Magician now stood in the second tier, one row back near the center. It was as if he'd been there all along, yet the patrons around him could not fathom his appearance there. The crowd all applauded as he bowed in equal respect.

"I thank you all for coming this evening. I hope you have enjoyed my theatricals and I hope I have challenged your sense of reality. Remember that belief is just an illusion that you create to distinguish that which is real from that which is unreal. Farewell and adieu."

And with his last word there was an explosive flash where the Magician stood. As the smoke cleared, the Magician was gone. From amongst the crowd, he'd simply vanished into thin air. The crowd, still standing, applauded one last time as the stage curtains closed and the lighting around the theatre came on gently, indicating the show was at its end.

But there was one person missing from the audience besides the Magician. The man with the handkerchief had disappeared during the act. Such was the excitement of the moment that not even the patrons in the adjoining seats thought to question his whereabouts. They were still unsure who had been sitting next to them through the rest of the show.

The mesmerized audience slowly made their way out of the theatre in jubilant merriment. After an evening of enchantment and delight, they now returned to reality: content with the moment; ready to return to the reality of life outside the theatre.

Chapter 8

The Two-Faced Man

*W*hen I finally awoke the next morning, it ended up being a mad dash for the train. I would have had the opportunity to make my way to the train station in a sensible fashion but my overuse of the snooze button had progressively removed that option. As I finally made my way onto the train and sat down I let out a sigh of relief, mixed with a reasonable amount of sheer exhaustion.

While I'd flown to Edinburgh on a one-way cheap fare, I'd decided to train back to London by myself for something different. I hadn't seen too much of England while living in London, which I was a little embarrassed about, and this was my way of seeing a bit more.

It wasn't crowded, why would it be at 7 a.m. on a Sunday morning? No, now that I was in a position to absorb my surroundings, it was clear that the world around me had not woken yet. The streets had been empty, the station quiet, but for some station workers and one or two delivery men setting bales of newspapers by a closed store front.

The train carriage was empty as well, but for an isolated passenger at the far end and myself. The air was chilled; the atmosphere, tranquil. I had awoken while the rest of the world was still in hibernation.

As the train pulled gently out of the platform, I looked out the window and said farewell and thank-you as the large "Edinburg" station placard passed me by. Is it possible to have gratitude towards a town? I don't know, but that's how I was feeling as we slowly made our way out of town into open country side.

What was I thankful for? For the good time? For the fun moments? For saving a lost soul? Or was I grateful for the enlightenment? I was grateful for it all.

It wasn't long before the drinks cart came by and I purchased myself a large coffee and some fruit. As I sat there having breakfast, trying to wake myself up, I wondered why I felt a such a strong and sudden sense of accomplishment.

As Edinburgh disappeared behind me into memory, that's what I felt. It was strange, but I felt like I'd achieved something. I'd done it. I'd found my way out of my lost and dejected state and now I felt, well, I guess I felt normal.

So why should I feel so proud of myself? What was so grand about my experience in Edinburgh that should warrant this sense of achievement? It wasn't like I was making myself feel this way intentionally; it's just what I remember feeling at the time.

I chuckled to myself as I sipped on the last of my coffee. Yes, it had been an adventure. Without knowing how or why,

I'd faced my demons and had come out a better and happier person. It was definitely comical. What kind of an adventure was it achieving normality? While the meaning was unclear to me, it still felt good.

When I thought about it some more, I felt like I was the first to discover my own mind. Before Edinburgh, I was unable to find meaning in my life. I think through discovering how my mind worked I was able to resolve this emptiness.

My life now had meaning because I understood who I was — or at least how my mind worked. I smirked at my own silliness as I gazed out the window. Yes, there were many great people who had made world-changing discoveries throughout the history of mankind. I, on the other hand, had discovered ME.

As my thoughts floated through the passing scenery, it became clear to me that who I was and how my mind worked were in fact separate concepts. My identity, or "who I was," could only be based upon an accumulation of my beliefs, whereas "how my mind worked" appeared to be more about how my beliefs affected me as I interacted with my environment.

So I'd found an elevated state of happiness based upon a new system of understanding how my mind worked, which was, in fact, a new-found belief. It seemed that not only had I changed in personality but also in functionality. These newfound ideas were re-constructing my mind with each new day. My mind felt elevated as the train passed through the countryside.

Could the mind really be explained by seemingly simple mathematical principles? That was the real question that I had on my mind: was my experience real or was it just my way of saving my mind from its troubled state? Surely, if our thoughts and actions can be explained by these statements, as it seemed so far, then they must be real. I know I believed in them … but would anyone else?

As the train glided through the rolling green hills, I wondered whether these new ideas would come with me to London or whether they'd remain in Edinburgh as if trapped in a dream that existed only within a moment in time.

What did it matter? I was relaxed and content, happy in the knowledge that everything ahead of me would be alright. I couldn't wait to get home now. Holidays are wonderful, but nothing beats getting home and crashing on your very own sofa. It wouldn't have mattered if I'd stayed in the fanciest hotel in Edinburgh; there's just something special about returning to your own little place filled with your own brand of creature comforts.

As I travelled back to London by train, I had plenty of time to get a new perspective on my new perspective. I mean, I'd spent all my time in Edinburgh discovering this new perspective on life. Now that I was away from the influences of Edinburgh, I had time to think about the meaning of this new perspective I'd acquired and make sure I was happy with it.

While I sat there gazing out the window, watching the landscape speed by, I wondered about the dramatic transformation I'd experienced. So much had happened in such a short time. I'd been so depressed for so long. I've said that I'd lost meaning in life, but now I understood that what I'd lost was the ability to evaluate what was important and what wasn't.

If we don't understand the value of our actions or the importance of our beliefs, then how can we determine or establish any validity in our actions in life?

In the period of my life before Edinburgh, I think I'd lost the people around me that had given meaning to my life. I lived my life finding meaning through those around me rather than through establishing meaning from within. Whereas now I felt that if I understood self then I must be able to establish meaning based on my own self-generated principles. With a little help from my friend the Magician, of course.

My weakness, my hopeless mental state, and my depression, had been created as I lost certain people in my life; trapped, alone and isolated in a foreign city. I'd progressively lost beliefs that had been dependent on my association with these people, with friends, family, and my community. It was other people who had impressed upon me their beliefs.

Little had I known that I'd acquired meaning in my life through assimilating other people's beliefs; a dependency on society that I didn't understand until I was free from the security it provided.

Once I'd lost these bonds I'd found myself stripped of purpose, naked and vulnerable to the ideas and beliefs of others; easily pushed from one belief to another as those around me sought to affirm their own beliefs.

Now, well, now I was different. I felt reborn, I felt alive. Somehow, the Magician had seeded an idea within my mind, and it was finally beginning to take root and grow. It wasn't like I assumed that I fully understood his principles; it was more that I felt like I could, through the application of these new principles, determine my own path through life.

Up until Edinburgh, my compass had been set by others. Now I was free to set my own course through life. I now had the means to navigate through life where ever it may lead me.

Yes, I'd reached a turning point in my life and was now moving in the direction I wanted. Don't get me wrong, I'm not saying that I'd made some resolute life goals that I would aspire to. I mean, I was still young, I didn't know what I wanted to do with my life — but I now looked forward to the uncertainty of my future rather than feeling that I could not face it.

Whatever direction I was moving in, it was the right one because I now understood how my mind worked in some very basic fashion and this new belief had redefined who I was.

My actions now had meaning and purpose. It wasn't that I now possessed a specific course for my life to take. Rather, I now possessed my own compass to determine which course to take through life. Through an understanding of the "how" I could choose the "why."

I was a new man. But what was I to do with these new ideas that I'd discovered with the help of my friends? I think there was a reason why I didn't discuss my adventure with Simon while hanging out with him in Edinburgh. There was a reason why I didn't discuss my experience with my family at the time or in the years to come.

I think it was a similar reason that prevented me from dealing with my personal misery of the previous years. I was afraid of losing my sense of certainty. In this instance, I was afraid of self-analysis or at least self-criticism. I was afraid of the criticism of others. I was afraid of what others might say to my new ideas.

Maybe they would like them or maybe they would discredit them instead. How vulnerable was this new self-belief to the assertions of others? Maybe everything I believed I'd accomplished was all in my head. Maybe I was just another crackpot.

I don't know if I really wanted to think about it too much. How often do we really look within ourselves and question our beliefs and motives? I don't think people like to interrogate themselves or delve too deeply into the nature of their own thoughts and actions. I think we'd rather be oblivious to our flaws.

As we go through life, we find certainty in our ideas and perceptions and cling onto that certainty as much as we can. We are naturally drawn to that which re-affirms our sense of certainty. We want to live in a reality where we do not have to face our fears, our weaknesses, or our insecurities.

We know they exist but rather than facing them, we hide from them. We believe our way away from them. We wrap ourselves in beliefs that prevent these uncertainties from getting in the way of our desire for more certainty. So, to share my discoveries would be to risk having them laughed at or rejected. No one ever talked to me about their own minds. No one ever came to me and said "I wonder what drives our emotions; I wonder how the mind works?"

Yes, to share these new beliefs was to risk having them stolen from me and replaced with the insecurities I'd been bathing in for too long. That idea scared the hell out of me.

Even if these new theories were in some way valid, why would anyone be interested in some twenty-something's ideas on how the mind works or what drives our emotions? I had no education in philosophy or psychology. Who was I to profess knowledge of such abstract notions?

No one goes out with friends and sits down to discuss the roots of their thoughts and feelings. I was reticent to speak with even my closest friends about my Edinburgh adventure. I'd never been in a situation like Edinburgh where anyone had cared to share such ideas. I guess people feel that they need a third party to analyze their minds rather than risking honest self-analysis.

We pay psychologists or psychiatrists to help us analyze our thoughts behind closed doors. Why is that, I wonder? Are we embarrassed with these apparent weaknesses? Are we afraid of how people will judge us if we share these deep secrets? Why are we so reactionary in our approach to understanding self? Why do we choose to understand everything around us before turning the magnifying glass towards self?

As I sat there on the train, I decided to continue to keep my ideas to myself. I decided that I would continue with my research but only share my ideas with Rob, my friend, the engineer, who genuinely understood.

While this process of self-analysis had been ignited by the chance meeting with the Magician, it was with the engineer that I now felt that I could confide with safely, without judgment or negativity. No, I wasn't confident enough to share these strangely simple new ideas with friends and family, let alone anyone else.

As the countryside drifted by, my thoughts continued to wander. I gazed out the window, looking over the rich green pastures and farmlands of England. I imagined the Magician perched high up on one of the rolling hills looking down on me. I could hear his voice as he shared his wisdom with me, each word permanently embedded in my mind; his ideas now sewn into the fabric of my thoughts.

He was present in my thoughts even when he wasn't present. The image was so clear within my mind. I could almost see the Magician's face looking back at me, chuckling away until the window went black as the train passed into a small tunnel … and he was gone.

We were pulling into another station and I watched as a few more weekend travelers joined the train. It was now mid-morning and a much more sensible hour to be hopping on a train. I heard the interior carriage door slide open and closed behind my seat as several people moved about the train.

One of the new passengers had the same youthful scruffiness as the engineer. I could almost have mistaken him for my friend from a distance. I wondered what the engineer would be doing today. I couldn't recall if he was working, but it was the weekend so it would make sense. I missed the guy already.

He had a way of making sense of things that I truly admired. He seemed so content in life. It had only been a few days since we met, but I felt like we had a true and solid friendship. But as the train accelerated toward London, I reminded myself that it was just me on the train returning to my real life in London.

As the train sped into London, the carriage jostled back and forth before entering one, last tunnel on its final approach into the station. As my life in London approached, too, I tried to hold onto my recent experiences. I imagined I could see the engineer and the Magician in the reflection of the glass. First I would see the Magician in the window looking back at me with his mysterious eyes before a tunnel light would flash into view.

Then I would see the engineer's face looking back with open sincerity and interest before another light would blind my sight. I could see each of their faces in the window alternating as the lights in the tunnel flashed by.

They were both so clear and distinct as they passed one

after the other. But as the train approached the London terminal platform and slowed down to a crawl, their images became less distinct. Their features blended until there was only one face looking back at me.

I'd arrived back into the big city reality of London. When the train finally came to a complete stop, the only reflection I saw in the window was my own.

Chapter VIII

Behind the Curtain

*A*s the Engineer tried to get his bearings in the darkness, he struggled to understand what had just happened. Only moments ago, he'd been watching the Magician seemingly disappear into thin air under his cloak and hat and then, inexplicably, he'd been transported to another location in what felt like an instant.

As the lighting around the theatre came back on, he stood up and started to look around. The sound of people from the audience indicated that he was still in the theatre, but the sound was muffled. The sound of the audience cheering seemed to come from the other side of the stage curtains.

He looked around to see if there was someone who could help him in his confused state. Soon, he could hear patrons leaving the theatre through the stage curtains in front of him. He was alone in the backstage area and everyone else was going home.

As he looked around, it was apparent that he was standing amongst some contraptions that the Magician had been using during the show. Now that he was up close, he could see many details that were not visible from the audience; items that had been covered during the show were now in plain sight.

How he would love to inspect them further! There were a variety of mechanical devices. What tickled the Engineer's curiosity was that some of them actually looked familiar. As he looked at them, he experienced a strong sense of déjà vu.

"Good evening," said the Magician as he suddenly appeared by the Engineer's side.

"Oh, hello," responded the Engineer, shocked and surprise by the Magician's sudden appearance and putting down the item he'd just picked up. "I'm a huge fan! This really is a pleasure."

"The pleasure is mine, I assure you," replied the Magician sincerely, bowing as he spoke.

At this point, both men looked at each other inquisitively. They were both familiar with the other, yet neither was confident on the details of their relationship.

The Engineer knew the Magician only from his performances each week. For many years now, he'd come to the shows and watched with delight. The Magician was a master of his trade and always brought the crowd to their feet with his various stunts of trickery and deception. He enjoyed playing with the crowd and challenging them.

The Magician only recognized the Engineer as a familiar face within the crowd; he knew that he was different from other patrons, but he didn't understand how. But that is why he'd brought him backstage. Tonight he would solve this riddle once and for all.

"It was another great show tonight," said the Engineer after a long pause. "I am a little curious how I got here though. Was that part of the show?"

"Yes and no," he answered. "I could have taken a patron from any seat in the audience. Yet I wanted to see the theatre from your seat in particular. You're a 'regular,' I think. Tell me, why do you come to my shows?" he asked as he moved around the stage, packing things away as he went, progressively covering up all the curiosities that had caught the Engineer's attention.

"I guess I've always been fascinated by magic," the Engineer responded. "I have always strived to understand how things work and yet magic presents itself in such a way that I cannot grasp. Tonight for example, I was sitting in my seat and then the next moment I was here. I wish I could understand this, yet I can't," he said, trying not to speak too much in his current state of excitement.

However, as the Magician picked up the lid to one of the crates that he was packing, the Engineer's expression changed.

"That box has my marking on it. It is the same as on the handkerchief I received tonight from your lovely assistant," exclaimed the Engineer.

"Ha," chuckled the Magician. "No, that is my insignia. The emblem is an M for Magician," he explained, taking the handkerchief from the Engineer's pocket and inspecting it for a moment before placing it back.

"This," he said, touching the box in front of him. "This is one of the devices I use for my shows. It bears my marking on it as with many of my props."

After the Engineer had paused for a moment, he let out a chuckle of his own as the mystery began to unfold.

"But if you turn the lid on its side the M becomes an E. I think I may have designed some of the devices that you use for your performances. I remember burning my letter into the lid. There cannot be another like it, as I made it myself."

The Magician paused for some time as he contemplated the meaning of this. He'd never questioned the source of the boxes as he'd taken possession of them. He'd merely requested them based on their purpose and used them based on their success in previous performances. Of course, there must be a designer. E for Engineer. So, this man was the engineer behind the devices!

If only for a moment, everything made sense as the two relative strangers looked eye-to-eye and finally, fully, understood one another. They finally understood their connection. Even though their worlds were entirely alien to each other — entirely separate — they were connected through their arts. They were in a symbiotic relationship with an entity that they had never been aware of. A glimmer of respect was apparent in the Magician's eyes. But, the connection was broken as he changed his tone:

"The riddle is solved, so now it is time for you to leave. Thank you for your services, but I am a man whose profession is built on secrecy and I, too, must leave this place shortly. Please show yourself out," he finished curtly as he turned to leave in the opposite direction.

"But I have so many questions," blurted out the Engineer. "Surely, you share my desire to understand how my designs work?"

"You know," responded the Magician as he turned to face the Engineer, "I have never allowed anyone to look at what takes place behind the stage curtains. It is not a place for any of the patrons, certainly not for someone insightful like yourself. It is a rule of mine that I have broken on this singular occasion. And I see now the great risk I have taken," he said, pausing to collect his thoughts.

"Do you know how I measure the success of my performance? It is through the reactions of the audience. Do they smile? Do they laugh? Do their eyes light up with amazement and wonder? Do they sit and applaud or do they stand? I do not need to understand your devices and how they work. It only matters whether I can use them to please the audience."

Again he paused, trying to capture the right words.

"You know, magic doesn't exist where there is understanding and I guess engineering doesn't exist without understanding. If you're to enjoy my arts and my unique talent, then it must be as part of the audience. Similarly, it is only from behind the curtains that I can practice my arts and provide entertainment for all my dear patrons. I'm afraid that is the very nature of our existence. And on that note, I must bid you goodnight and farewell."

The Magician bowed courteously and exited through an opening at one side of the curtains. The Engineer shrugged to himself as he found his own way out of the theatre, his mind still filled with unanswered questions.

What a curious evening it had been; delightful, yet not without intrigue. He'd been on the brink of understanding so much, only to be turned away, in the end, by the Magician.

As he stepped out onto the street he looked down and

noticed the handkerchief still sticking out of his pocket. He hadn't been given an opportunity to ask the Magician why it had been placed there by the assistant.

Maybe the Magician had used it as a marker so he could identify him in the audience. To the Engineer though, it would make a nice memento of this unusual and wondrous evening.

As he took it from his pocket to inspect it more closely he found, as he unraveled it, that there was a message written on it. A message, he was certain, that had not been there when initially placed in his pocket. One last magic trick! He read it silently to himself:

"All actions are taken to increase certainty" M

He placed the handkerchief back into his pocket and as he meandered home through the city streets he pondered these words. What on earth could they possibly mean?

Back in the theatre, there was little activity in the foyer or grand auditorium. All was quiet except for some cleaning staff that were slowly working their way through each row of seats. The stage curtains were closed, with little activity behind them, either.

There was one room in the dark recesses of the theatre, however, that was out of sight — but not out of mind. It was a storage room deep in the backstage area. There were no people there; only boxes. To say there were boxes would be to understate the number of boxes that sat piled up on top of each other.

The room was enormous and filled to the top in some places with boxes of various sizes. There was no regularity in the size of the boxes; each one appeared different. The room was dark, with no need for lighting, but if one was to illuminate this vast cavern filled with boxes, something quite odd might be seen.

The boxes were *moving*.

Some of them were creeping from one place to another, quite slowly. Others tumbled from one location to another. There were boxes that shrank into themselves and some that swelled up as if something inside them struggled to gain more space. Even stranger yet, some boxes simply disappeared entirely as regularly as new boxes blinked into existence.

Many of the boxes were marked with the Magician's M or possibly the Engineer's E. But among the multitude of boxes, one small box sat patiently waiting. It didn't move. It didn't change. It sat in the dark recesses of the theatre like a seed in a garden waiting for the right time to grow. It was marked with its own unique marking burnt into the wooden crate

In the room at the back of the stage behind the curtains, the mysterious and seemingly uncoordinated chaos continued in complete darkness. With no doors in or out of the room, its secrets remained trapped by the frailty of their own inherent existence; naked to the reality that existed outside of the theater.

Conclusion

*I*t was back in Edinburgh many years ago when one of the locals that I'd just met said to me: "the way you know that you've lost your mind is that you can't find it."

I remember being caught off guard. I felt, more than understood, the underlying suggestion of a riddle that I couldn't frame correctly. Is there a difference between something being lost and an inability to find it? I'm sure they were smiling when they provided me with these dubious words of wisdom. But for some reason, the words stuck with me and teased my mind. I needed to understand.

While most of my memories from that night long ago have been lost in time, that brief encounter with a relative stranger stayed with me. Many important details from my life history seem to have evaporated through the bars of whatever vault they were stored, regardless of my desire to keep hold of them.

But this seemingly meaningless conundrum remained trapped in my mind, unsolved; lost in a maze without entrance or exit. Like the countless riddles we perceive in life and yet are unable, for whatever reason, to solve.

It wasn't just the language they'd used that teased my mind.

It was also, and maybe more importantly, the realization that I didn't understand my own mind. Why was I so ignorant about an aspect of my life that could not be more central to the core of my existence?

The mind is not an easy thing to define or discuss, let alone explain. We know it exists because we experience our life as part of it. We know, or presume, that it is an aspect of the brain. But it's not something we can define based on its appearance or function as easily as other body parts such as the heart or the lungs, for example. There's no diagram in medical text books that has an arrow that points to an area inside our skull indicating the location of "The Mind."

Even when we haven't lost our mind, we still can't say exactly where it is. It's a rather abstract aspect of our existence and yet it's at the center of everything we do. Or maybe I should say that we're at the center of everything it does.

Its existence is something that we have determined or defined based on a need to define self. So, through our need to define and understand self, we have postulated rather than proven the existence of "the mind." We know it exists because we exist — "I think therefore I am."

But as to its location or to the details of how it works, there, we become a little less sure of ourselves. The existence of the mind is abstract by its very nature — so finding one's mind after it's lost must be more difficult when we live our lives not knowing where it was in the first place.

That being said, my tale isn't about how I lost my mind, as you can see, but rather, how I found it. In my quest for meaning in life I discovered how to understand myself. I was able to delve beneath the thick blanket of chaos that we so often use to protect ourselves through life and see how truly simple it is to understand self.

Put simply, I discovered a system for understanding my thoughts and actions and how they generate emotions based on the predictive or resultant effects of them.

What I discovered through continued self-analysis was a starting point or point of harmony for my mind. I created a new "first place." I discovered what it was that gave me certainty in life. I use this starting point as a beacon in times when chaos threatens to take over my mind. It is an anchor that I have used over many years to connect my past, present and future life.

We all experience emotions in waves that may gently collide with our conscious mind or crash upon it with such strength that we fear will destroy us. However, I found that if I could analyze my emotions then quite often I could bring my mind back to a point of harmony.

I also found that by understanding what changes influenced my certainty, I could prevent many negative emotions just through an awareness of change. I no longer feared — and I no longer fear — my emotions.

For much of my life, I'd been scared to venture into the uncertainty of my own mind for fear of losing my way. However, by creating a framework for understanding the mind I now have a tourist map to find my way around my own thoughts.

Our existence is something we only experience in the present. As such, we only experience our emotions in the present and yet, as they are dependent on change, they will always be tied to our past experiences or to our expectations regarding the future.

That means we can draw from our past experiences to determine our emotional state or we can look to the future. Regardless of whether our experiences in life have been good or bad we can't change them, they're history. What we can do is influence our future through our decisions in the present. Something many of us forget.

I have a friend who, regardless of the negative things that happen in her life, is always bubbling with happiness and enthusiasm. She doesn't dwell in the past. She doesn't let bad experiences put her in a bad mood. She lives for what *will* happen, rather than what *has* happened. We all have friends like this. We also have friends whose happiness or unhappiness is trapped in a history that will not change.

It cannot be denied that everything that has happened in your life has led you to this instant right now. Your past may be filled with wonder or woes, but it is immutable. If you allow your emotional state to be dependent on your past experiences, then you lose the freedom to enjoy the future. In other words, you can either stagnate in the past or fall in love with the future. It is our future that we should aspire to define us — not our past.

My journey to Edinburgh provided the impetus for me to discover my mind. For many years, I kept my ideas to myself. I kept my ideas and experiences somewhere in the recesses of my mind. I left them alone, hoping they would take deeper root and begin to grow; wondering whether they were illusion or real.

Yet with each experience my life brought to me, I enjoyed the ongoing wonder of how my theories helped me make sense of my experiences. My understanding of self helped me to understand my feelings, both good and bad. It helped me deal with the bad and enjoy the good.

Everything that I share with you has stemmed from the humorous quandary propositioned to me by a stranger in Edinburgh that made one simple question resonate within me: Why don't I understand how my mind works? I'd been trapped, a prisoner of my own mind; confined by my ignorance. But with the discovery of one simple idea, given to me by a stranger on one, windy afternoon, I had the key to true self-awareness.

An idea is but the seed from which a belief can grow. An idea is like an invisible present without wrapping or protection from reality. A belief is more sturdy; framed in certainty and wrapped in the truth of experience. Over the years, my fragile ideas have grown and evolved naturally into beliefs — not through magic, but through experience.

Magic, on the other hand, is where our beliefs collide before our eyes; where we juxtapose the possible with the impossible. It is where we strip back the absolute belief in reality and challenge our certainty. There are many illusions in what we refer to as reality. Most of us live our entire lives believing that the mind is an unsolvable mystery.

What if your mind wasn't an enigma rather a library of logic waiting to be understood? Or maybe a classic theatre with all its grandeur filled with art, beauty and magic? Would you be brave enough to peer behind the stage curtain? Would you be bold enough to delve into the backstage area and explore its hidden treasures?

What if you could look inside yourself and finally understand the circus caravan that carries you through life? Would you shy away from looking into the crystal ball or would you stare into its depths and enjoy the show?

The End